William Wymark Jacobs

Sea Urchins

ISBN/EAN: 9783337001841

Printed in Europe, USA, Canada, Australia, Japan

Cover: Foto ©Andreas Hilbeck / pixelio.de

More available books at **www.hansebooks.com**

SEA URCHINS

MANY CARGOES

Crown 8vo. 3s. 6d.

"I have just been reading *Many Cargoes*, by Mr. W. W. Jacobs, which has made me laugh much and often. It is a collection of short stories, reprinted from various periodicals, and dealing with men who go down to the sea in ships of moderate tonnage; stories told with such fresh and unforced fun that *their drollery is perfectly irresistible.* I have never heard of Mr. W. W. Jacobs before, and for anything I know this may be his first literary voyage, but I can only say that the sooner he puts to sea again and brings back more cargoes of the same goods the better I shall be pleased."—*Punch.*

"When a bachelor with a healthy appetite takes up a book in the club reading-room, after a hard day's work, and suddenly discovers that it is ten o'clock, that he has forgotten all about his dinner, and that he is too sore in the ribs to enjoy it, one may fairly argue that the book has merits of a peculiar order. A similar conclusion may be drawn from the confession of an ardent golfer in the course of a railway journey to a favourite Surrey green, that if he read any more of the same book it would 'put him off his stroke.' For the authenticity of these two incidents the present reviewer is prepared to vouch, and hastens, for the benefit of all those who have not made the acquaintance of the volume in question, to state that its name is *Many Cargoes*, a collection of short stories of seafaring life by W. W. Jacobs, an author who, to judge from his first essay, is as richly equipped with the sense of the ludicrous as any writer now before the public."—*Spectator.*

LAWRENCE & BULLEN, Ltd.

16, Henrietta Street, Covent Garden, London

William Wymark Jacobs

Sea Urchins

SEA URCHINS

BY

W. W. JACOBS

AUTHOR OF "MANY CARGOES," "THE SKIPPER'S WOOING"
ETC. ETC.

LONDON
LAWRENCE AND BULLEN, LTD.
16, HENRIETTA STREET, COVENT GARDEN
1898

TO MY SISTER FLORENCE

CONTENTS

	PAGE
SMOKED SKIPPER	I
A SAFETY MATCH	23
A RASH EXPERIMENT	44
THE CABIN PASSENGER	67
"CHOICE SPIRITS"	78
A DISCIPLINARIAN	106
BROTHER HUTCHINS	117
THE DISBURSEMENT SHEET	130
RULE OF THREE	147
PICKLED HERRING	160
TWO OF A TRADE	169
AN INTERVENTION	190
THE GREY PARROT	201
MONEY-CHANGERS	222
THE LOST SHIP	234

SEA URCHINS

SMOKED SKIPPER

"WAPPING Old Stairs?" said the rough individual, shouldering the bran-new sea-chest, and starting off at a trot with it; "yus, I know the place, captin. Fust v'y'ge, sir?"

"Ay, ay, my hearty," replied the owner of the chest, a small, ill-looking lad of fourteen. "Not so fast with those timbers of yours. D'ye hear?"

"All right, sir," said the man, and, slackening his pace, twisted his head round to take stock of his companion.

"This ain't your fust v'y'ge, captin," he said admiringly; "don't tell me. I could twig that directly I see you. Ho, what's the use o' trying to come it over a poor 'ard-working man like that?"

"I don't think there's much about the sea I don't know," said the boy in a satisfied voice. "Starboard, starboard your hellum a bit."

B

'The man obeying promptly, they went the remainder of the distance in this fashion, to the great inconvenience of people coming from the other direction.

"And a cheap 'arf-crown's worth, too, captin," said the man, as he put the chest down at the head of the stairs and thoughtfully sat on it pending payment.

"I want to go off to the *Susan Jane*," said the boy, turning to a waterman who was sitting in his boat, holding on to the side of the steps with his hand.

"All right," said the man, "give us a hold o' your box."

"Put it aboard," said the boy to the other man.

"A' right, captin," said the man, with a cheerful smile, "but I'll 'ave my 'arf-crown fust if you don't mind."

"But you said sixpence at the station," said the boy.

"*Two* an' sixpence, captin," said the man, still smiling, "but I'm a bit 'usky, an' p'raps you didn't hear the two—'arf a crown 's the regler price. We ain't allowed to do it under."

"Well, I won't tell anybody," said the boy.

"Give the man 'is 'arf-crown," said the waterman, with sudden heat; "that's 'is price, and my fare's eigh-teen pence."

"All right," said the boy readily; "cheap, too. I didn't know the price, that's all. But I can't pay either of you till I get aboard. I've only got sixpence. I'll tell the captain to give you the rest."

"Tell 'oo?" demanded the light-porter, with some violence.

"The captain," said the boy.

"Look 'ere, you give me that 'arf-crown," said the other, "else I'll chuck your box overboard, an' you after it."

"Wait a minute, then," said the boy, darting away up the narrow alley which led to the stairs; "I'll go and get change."

"'E's goin' to change 'arf a suvren, or p'raps a suvren," said the waterman; "you'd better make it five bob, matey."

"Ah, an' you make yours more," said the light-porter cordially. "Well, I'm—— Well of all the——"

"Get off that box," said the big policeman who had come back with the boy. "Take your six-pence an' go. If I catch you down this way again——"

He finished the sentence by taking the fellow by the scruff of the neck and giving him a violent push as he passed him.

"Waterman's fare is threepence," he said to the

boy, as the man in the boat, with an utterly expressionless face, took the chest from him. "I'll stay here till he has put you aboard."

The boy took his seat, and the waterman, breathing hard, pulled out towards the vessels in the tier. He looked at the boy and then at the figure on the steps, and, apparently suppressing a strong inclination to speak, spat violently over the side.

"Fine big chap, ain't he?" said the boy.

The waterman, affecting not to hear, looked over his shoulder, and pulled strongly with his left towards a small schooner, from the deck of which a couple of men were watching the small figure in the boat.

"That's the boy I was going to tell you about," said the skipper, "and remember this 'ere ship's a pirate."

"It's got a lot o' pirates aboard of it," said the mate fiercely, as he turned and regarded the crew, "a set o' lazy, loafing, idle, worthless——"

"It's for the boy's sake," interrupted the skipper.

"Where'd you pick him up?" inquired the other.

"He's the son of a friend o' mine what I've brought aboard to oblige," replied the skipper. "He's got a fancy for being a pirate, so just to oblige his father I told him we was a pirate. He wouldn't have come if I hadn't."

"I'll pirate him," said the mate, rubbing his hands.

"He's a dreadful 'andful, by all accounts," continued the other; "got his 'ed stuffed full o' these 'ere penny dreadfuls till they've turned his brain almost. He started by being an Indian, and goin' off on 'is own with two other kids. When 'e wanted to turn cannibal the other two objected, and gave 'im in charge. After that he did a bit o' burgling, and it cost 'is old man no end o' money to hush it up."

"Well, what did *you* want him for?" grumbled the mate.

"I'm goin' to knock the nonsense out of him," said the skipper softly, as the boat grazed the side. "Just step for'ard and let the hands know what's expected of 'em. When we get to sea it won't matter."

The mate moved off grumbling, as the small fare stood on the thwarts and scrambled up over the side. The waterman passed up the chest, and dropping the coppers into his pocket, pushed off again without a word.

"Well, you've got here all right, Ralph?" said the skipper. "What do you think of her?"

"She's a rakish-looking craft," said the boy, looking round the dingy old tub with much satisfaction; "but where's your arms?"

"Hush!" said the skipper, and laid his finger on his nose.

"Oh, all right," said the youth testily, "but you might tell *me*."

"You shall know all in good time," said the skipper patiently, turning to the crew, who came shuffling up, masking broad grins with dirty palms.

"Here's a new shipmate for you, my lads. He's small, but he's the right stuff."

The new-comer drew himself up, and regarded the crew with some dissatisfaction. For desperadoes they looked far too good-tempered and prone to levity.

"What's the matter with you, Jem Smithers?" inquired the skipper, scowling at a huge fair-haired man, who was laughing discordantly.

"I was thinkin' o' the last party I killed, sir," said Jem, with sudden gravity. "I allers laugh when I think 'ow he squealed."

"You laugh too much," said the other sternly, as he laid a hand on Ralph's shoulder. "Take a lesson from this fine feller; he don't laugh. He acts. Take 'im down below an' show him 'is bunk."

"Will you please to follow me, sir?" said Smithers, leading the way below. "I dessay you'll find it a bit stuffy, but that's owing to

Bill Dobbs. A regler old sea-dog is Bill, always sleeps in 'is clothes and never washes."

"I don't think the worse of him for that," said Ralph, regarding the fermenting Dobbs kindly.

"You'd best keep a civil tongue in your 'ed, my lad," said Dobbs shortly.

"Never mind 'im," said Smithers cheerfully; "nobody takes any notice o' old Dobbs. You can 'it 'im if you like. I won't let him hurt you."

"I don't want to start by quarrelling," said Ralph seriously.

"You're afraid," said Jem tauntingly; "you'll never make one of us. 'It 'im; I won't let him hurt you."

Thus aroused, the boy, first directing Dobbs' attention to his stomach by a curious duck of the head, much admired as a feint in his neighbourhood, struck him in the face. The next moment the forecastle was in an uproar and Ralph prostrate on Dobbs' knees, frantically reminding Jem of his promise.

"All right, I won't let him 'urt you," said Jem consolingly.

"But he *is* hurting me," yelled the boy. "He's hurting me *now*."

"Well, wait till I get 'im ashore," said Jem, "his old woman won't know him when I've done with him."

The boy's reply to this was a torrent of shrill abuse, principally directed to Jem's facial shortcomings.

"Now don't get rude," said the seaman, grinning.

"Squint-eyes," cried Ralph fiercely.

"When you've done with that 'ere young gentleman, Dobbs," said Jem, with exquisite politeness, "I should like to 'ave 'im for a little bit to teach 'im manners."

"'E don't want to go," said Dobbs, grinning, as Ralph clung to him. "He knows who's kind to him."

"Wait till I get a chance at you," sobbed Ralph, as Jem took him away from Dobbs.

"Lord lumme," said Jem, regarding him in astonishment. "Why, he's actooaly cryin'. I've seen a good many pirates in my time, Bill, but this is a new sort."

"Leave the boy alone," said the cook, a fat, good-natured man. "Here, come 'ere, old man. They don't mean no 'arm."

Glad to escape, Ralph made his way over to the cook, grinding his teeth with shame as that worthy took him between his knees and mopped his eyes with something which he called a handkerchief.

"You'll be all right," he said kindly. "You'll

be as good a pirate as any of us before you 've finished."

"Wait till the first engagement, that 's all," sobbed the boy. " If somebody don't get shot in the back it won't be my fault."

The two seamen looked at each other. " That 's wot hurt my 'and then," said Dobbs slowly. " I thought it was a jack-knife."

He reached over, and unceremoniously grabbing the boy by the collar, pulled him towards him, and drew a small cheap revolver from his pocket. " Look at that, Jem."

" Take your fingers orf the blessed trigger and then I will," said the other, somewhat sourly.

" I 'll pitch it overboard," said Dobbs.

" Don't be a fool, Bill," said Smithers, pocketing it, " that 's worth a few pints o' anybody's money. Stand out o' the way Bill, the Pirit King wants to go on deck."

Bill moved aside as the boy went to the ladder, and allowing him to get up four or five steps, did the rest for him with his shoulder. The boy reached the deck on all fours, and, regaining a more dignified position as soon as possible, went and leaned over the side, regarding with lofty contempt the busy drudges on wharf and river.

They sailed at midnight and brought up in

the early dawn in Longreach, where a lighter loaded with barrels came alongside, and the boy smelt romance and mystery when he learnt that they contained powder. They took in ten tons, the lighter drifted away, the hatches were put on, and they started once more.

It was his first voyage, and he regarded with eager interest the craft passing up and down. He had made his peace with the seamen, and they regaled him with blood-curdling stories of their adventures, in the vain hope of horrifying him.

"'E's a beastly little rascal, that's wot 'e is," said the indignant Bill, who had surprised himself by his powers of narration; "fancy larfin' when I told 'im of pitchin' the baby to the sharks."

"'E's all right, Bill," said the cook softly. "Wait till you've got seven of 'em."

"What are you doing here, boy?" demanded the skipper, as Ralph, finding the seamen's yarns somewhat lacking in interest, strolled aft with his hands in his pockets.

"Nothing," said the boy, staring.

"Keep the other end o' the ship," said the skipper sharply, "an' go an' 'elp the cook with the taters."

Ralph hesitated, but a grin on the mate's face decided him.

"I didn't come here to peel potatoes," he said loftily.

"Oh, indeed," said the skipper politely; "an' wot might you 'ave come for, if it ain't being too inquisitive?"

"To fight the enemy," said Ralph shortly.

"Come 'ere," said the skipper.

The boy came slowly towards him.

"Now look 'ere," said the skipper, "I'm going to try and knock a little sense into that stupid 'ed o' yours. I've 'eard all about your silly little games ashore. Your father said he couldn't manage you, so I'm goin' to have a try, and you'll find I'm a very different sort o' man to deal with to wot 'e is. The idea o' thinking this ship was a pirate. Why, a boy your age ought to know there ain't such things nowadays."

"You told me you was," said the boy hotly, "else I wouldn't have come."

"That's just why I told you," said the skipper. "But I didn't think you'd be such a fool as to believe it. Pirates, indeed! Do we look like pirates?"

"You don't," said the boy with a sneer; "you look more like——"

"Like wot?" asked the skipper, edging closer to him. "Eh, like wot?'

"I forget the word," said Ralph, with strong good sense.

"Don't tell any lies now," said the skipper, flushing, as he heard a chuckle from the mate. "Go on, out with it. I'll give you just two minutes."

"I forget it," persisted Ralph.

"Dustman?" suggested the mate, coming to his assistance. "Coster, chimbley - sweep, mudlark, pick-pocket, convict, washer-wom——"

"If you'll look after your dooty, George, instead o' interferin' in matters that don't concern you," said the skipper in a choking voice, "I shall be obliged. Now, then, you boy, what were you going to say I was like?"

"Like the mate," said Ralph slowly.

"Don't tell lies," said the skipper furiously; "you couldn't 'ave forgot that word."

"I didn't forget it," said Ralph, "but I didn't know how you'd like it."

The skipper looked at him dubiously, and pushing his cap from his brow scratched his head.

"And I didn't know how the mate 'ud like it, either," continued the boy.

He relieved the skipper from an awkward dilemma by walking off to the galley and starting on a bowl of potatoes. The master of the *Susan*

Jane watched him blankly for some time and then looked round at the mate.

"You won't get much change out of 'im," said the latter, with a nod; "insultin' little devil."

The other made no reply, but as soon as the potatoes were finished set his young friend to clean brass work, and after that to tidy the cabin up and help the cook clean his pots and pans. Meantime the mate went below and overhauled his chest.

"This is where he gets all them ideas from," he said, coming aft with a big bundle of penny papers. "Look at the titles of 'em—'The Lion of the Pacific,' 'The One-armed Buccaneer,' 'Captain Kidd's Last Voyage.'"

He sat down on the cabin skylight and began turning them over, and, picking out certain gems of phraseology, read them aloud to the skipper. The latter listened at first with scorn and then with impatience.

"I can't make head or tail out of what you're reading, George," he said snappishly. "Who was Rudolph? Read straight ahead."

Thus urged, the mate, leaning forward so that his listener might hear better, read steadily through a serial in the first three numbers. The third instalment left Rudolph swimming in a race with three sharks and a boat-load of cannibals; and the joint efforts of both men failed to discover the other numbers.

"Just wot I should 'ave expected of 'im," said the skipper, as the mate returned from a fruitless search in the boy's chest. "I'll make him a bit more orderly on this ship. Go an' lock them other things up in your drawer, George. He's not to 'ave 'em again."

The schooner was getting into open water now, and began to feel it. In front of them was the blue sea, dotted with white sails and funnels belching smoke, speeding from England to worlds of romance and adventure. Something of the kind the cook said to Ralph, and urged him to get up and look for himself. He also, with the best intentions, discussed the restorative properties of fat pork from a medical point of view.

The next few days the boy divided between sea-sickness and work, the latter being the skipper's great remedy for piratical yearnings. Three or four times he received a mild drubbing, and, what was worse than the drubbing, had to give an answer in the affirmative to the skipper's inquiry as to whether he felt in a more wholesome frame of mind. On the fifth morning they stood in towards Fairhaven, and to his great joy he saw trees and houses again.

They stayed at Fairhaven just long enough to put

out a small portion of their cargo, Ralph, stripped
to his shirt and trousers, having to work in the
hold with the rest, and proceeded to Lowport, a
little place some thirty miles distant, to put out
their powder.

It was evening before they arrived, and, the
tide being out, anchored in the mouth of the
river on which the town stands.

"Git in about four o'clock," said the skipper to
the mate, as he looked over the side towards the
little cluster of houses on the shore. "Do you
feel better now I've knocked some o' that nonsense out o' you, boy?"

"Much better, sir," said Ralph respectfully.

"Be a good boy," said the skipper, pausing on
the companion-ladder, "and you can stay with us
if you like. Better turn in now, as you'll have
to make yourself useful again in the morning
working out the cargo."

He went below, leaving the boy on deck. The
crew were in the forecastle smoking, with the
exception of the cook, who was in the galley
over a little private business of his own.

An hour later the cook went below to prepare
for sleep. The other two men were already in
bed, and he was about to get into his when he
noticed that Ralph's bunk, which was under his
own, was empty. He went up on deck and looked

round, and, returning below, scratched his nose in thought.

"Where's the boy?" he demanded, taking Jem by the arm and shaking him.

"Eh?" said Jem, rousing. "Whose boy?"

"Our boy, Ralph," said the cook. "I can't see 'im nowhere. I 'ope 'e ain't gone overboard, pore little chap."

Jem refusing to discuss the matter, the cook awoke Dobbs. Dobbs swore at him peacefully, and resumed his slumbers. The cook went up again and prowled round the deck, looking in all sorts of unlikely places for the boy. He even climbed a little way into the rigging, and, finding no traces of him, was reluctantly forced to the conclusion that he had gone overboard.

"Pore little chap," he said solemnly, looking over the ship's side at the still water.

He walked slowly aft, shaking his head, and looking over the stern, brought up suddenly with a cry of dismay and rubbed his eyes. The ship's boat had also disappeared.

"Wot?" said the two seamen as he ran below and communicated the news. "Well, if it's gorn, it's gorn."

"Hadn't I better go an' tell the skipper?" said the cook.

"Let 'im find it out 'isself," said Jem, purring

contentedly in the blankets. "It's 'is boat. Go' night."

"Time we 'ad a noo 'un too," said Dobbs, yawning. "Don't you worry your 'ed, cook, about what don't consarn you."

The cook took the advice, and, having made his few simple preparations for the night, blew out the lamp and sprang into his bunk. Then he uttered a sharp exclamation, and getting out again fumbled for the matches and relit the lamp. A minute later he awoke his exasperated friends for the third time.

"S'elp me, cook," began Jem fiercely.

"If you don't I will," said Dobbs, sitting up and trying to reach the cook with his clenched fist.

"It's a letter pinned to my pillow," said the cook in trembling tones, as he held it to the lamp.

"Well, we don't want to 'ear it," said Jem. "Shut up, d'ye hear?"

But there was that in the cook's manner which awed him.

"Dear cook," he read feverishly, "I have made an infernal machine with clockwork, and hid it in the hold near the gunpowder when we were at Fairhaven. I think it will go off between ten and eleven to-night, but I am not quite sure about the time. Don't tell those other beasts, but

jump overboard and swim ashore. I have taken
the boat. I would have taken you too, but you
told me you swam seven miles once, so you can
eas——"

The reading came to an abrupt termination as
his listeners sprang out of their bunks, and, bolting
on deck, burst wildly into the cabin, and breath-
lessly reeled off the heads of the letter to its
astonished occupants.

"Stuck a wot in the hold?" gasped the skipper.

"Infernal machine," said the mate; "one of
them things wot you blow up the 'Ouses of
Parliament with."

"Wot's the time now?" interrogated Jem
anxiously.

"'Bout ha'-past ten," said the cook trembling.
"Let's give 'em a hail ashore."

They leaned over the side, and sent a mighty
shout across the water. Most of Lowport had gone
to bed, but the windows in the inn were bright, and
lights showed in the upper windows of two or three
of the cottages.

Again they shouted in deafening chorus, casting
fearful looks behind them, and in the silence a faint
answering hail came from the shore. They shouted
again like madmen, until listening intently they
heard a boat's keel grate on the beach, and then
the welcome click of oars in the rowlocks

"Make haste," bawled Dobbs vociferously, as the boat came creeping out of the darkness. "W'y don't you make 'aste?"

"Wot's the row?" cried a voice from the boat.

"Gunpowder!" yelled the cook frantically; "there's ten tons of it aboard just going to explode. Hurry up."

The sound of the oars ceased and a startled murmur was heard from the boat; then an oar was pulled jerkily.

"They're putting back," said Jem suddenly. "I'm going to swim for it. Stand by to pick me up, mates," he shouted, and lowering himself with a splash into the water struck out strongly towards them.

Dobbs, a poor swimmer, after a moment's hesitation, followed his example.

"I can't swim a stroke," cried the cook, his teeth chattering.

The others, who were in the same predicament, leaned over the side, listening. The swimmers were invisible in the darkness, but their progress was easily followed by the noise they made. Jem was the first to be hauled on board, and a minute or two later the listeners on the schooner heard him assisting Dobbs. Then the sounds of strife, of thumps, and wicked words broke on their delighted ears.

"They're coming back for us," said the mate, taking a deep breath. "Well done, Jem."

The boat came towards them, impelled by powerful strokes, and was soon alongside. The three men tumbled in hurriedly, their fall being modified by the original crew, who were lying crouched up in the bottom of the boat. Jem and Dobbs gave way with hearty goodwill, and the doomed ship receded into the darkness. A little knot of people had gathered on the shore, and, receiving the tidings, became anxious for the safety of their town. It was felt that the windows, at least, were in imminent peril, and messengers were hastily sent round to have them opened.

Still the deserted *Susan Jane* made no sign. Twelve o'clock struck from the little church at the back of the town, and she was still intact.

Something's gone wrong," said an old fisherman with a bad way of putting things. "Now's the time for somebody to go and tow her out to sea."

There was no response.

"To save Lowport," said the speaker feelingly. "If I was only twenty years younger——"

"It's old men's work," said a voice.

The skipper, straining his eyes through the gloom in the direction of his craft, said nothing. He began to think that she had escaped after all.

Two o'clock struck, and the crowd began to disperse. Some of the bolder inhabitants who were fidgety about draughts closed their windows, and children who had been routed out of their beds to take a nocturnal walk inland were led slowly back. By three o'clock the danger was felt to be over, and day broke and revealed the forlorn *Susan Jane* still riding at anchor.

" I 'm going aboard," said the skipper suddenly ; "who 's coming with me ? "

Jem and the mate and the town policeman volunteered, and, borrowing the boat which had served them before, pulled swiftly out to their vessel, and, taking the hatches off with unusual gentleness, commenced their search. It was nervous work at first, but they became inured to it, and, moreover, a certain suspicion, slight at first, but increasing in intensity as the search proceeded, gave them some sense of security. Later still they began to eye each other shamefacedly.

" I don't believe there 's anything there," said the policeman, sitting down and laughing boisterously ; "that boy 's been making a fool of you."

" That 's about the size of it," groaned the mate. " We 'll be the laughing-stock o' the town."

The skipper, who was standing with his back towards him, said nothing ; but, peering about, stooped suddenly, and, with a sharp exclamation, picked up something from behind a damaged case.

"I've got it," he yelled suddenly; "stand clear!"

He scrambled hastily on deck, and, holding his find at arm's length, with his head averted, flung it far into the water. A loud cheer from a couple of boats which were watching greeted his action, and a distant response came from the shore.

"Was that a infernal machine?" whispered the bewildered Jem to the mate. "Why, it looked to me just like one o' them tins o' corned beef."

The mate shook his head at him and glanced at the constable, who was gazing longingly over the side. "Well, I've 'eard of people being killed by *them* sometimes," he said with a grin.

A SAFETY MATCH

M R. BOOM, late of the mercantile marine, had the last word, but only by the cowardly expedient of getting out of earshot of his daughter first, and then hurling it at her with a voice trained to compete with hurricanes. Miss Boom avoided a complete defeat by leaning forward with her head on one side in the attitude of an eager but unsuccessful listener, a pose which she abandoned for one of innocent joy when her sire, having been deluded into twice repeating his remarks, was fain to relieve his overstrained muscles by a fit of violent coughing.

"I b'lieve she heard it all along," said Mr. Boom sourly, as he continued his way down the winding lane to the little harbour below. "The only way to live at peace with wimmen is to always be at sea; then they make a fuss of you when you come home—if you don't stay too long, that is."

He reached the quay, with its few tiny cottages, and brown nets spread about to dry in the sun, and walking up and down, grumbling, regarded with jaundiced eye a few small smacks which lay in the harbour, and two or three crusted amphibians lounging aimlessly about.

"Mornin', Mr. Boom," said a stalwart youth in sea-boots, appearing suddenly over the edge of the quay from his boat.

"Mornin', Dick," said Mr. Boom affably; "just goin' off?"

"'Bout an hour's time," said the other; "Miss Boom well, sir?"

"She's a' right," said Mr. Boom; "me an' her 've just had a few words. She picked up something off the floor what she said was a cake o' mud off my heel. Said she wouldn't have it," continued Mr. Boom, his voice rising. "My own floor too. Swep' it up off the floor with a dustpan and brush, and held it in front of me to look at."

Dick Tarrell gave a grunt which might mean anything—Mr. Boom took it for sympathy.

"I called her old maid," he said with gusto; "'you're a fidgety old maid,' I said. You should ha' seen her look. Do you know what I think, Dick?"

"Not exactly," said Tarrell cautiously.

"I b'leeve she's that savage that she'd take the first man that asked her," said the other triumphantly; "she's sitting up there at the door of the cottage, all by herself."

Tarrell sighed.

"With not a soul to speak to," said Mr. Boom pointedly.

The other kicked at a small crab which was passing, and returned it to its native element in sections.

"I'll walk up there with you if you're going that way," he said at length.

"No, I'm just having a look round," said Mr. Boom, "but there's nothing to hinder you going, Dick, if you've a mind to."

"There's no little thing you want, as I'm going there, I s'pose?" suggested Tarrell. "It's awkward when you go there and say, 'Good-morning,' and the girl says, 'Good-morning,' and then you don't say any more and she don't say any more. If there was anything you wanted that I could help her look for, it 'ud make talk easier."

"Well—go for my baccy pouch," said Mr. Boom, after a minute's thought, "it'll take you a long time to find that."

"Why?" inquired the other.

"'Cos I've got it here," said the unscrupulous Mr. Boom, producing it, and placidly filling his pipe. "You might spend—ah—the best part of an hour looking for that."

He turned away with a nod, and Tarrell, after
looking about him in a hesitating fashion to
make sure that his movements were not attract-
ing the attention his conscience told him they
deserved, set off in the hang-dog fashion peculiar
to nervous lovers up the road to the cottage.
Kate Boom was sitting at the door as her
father had described, and, in apparent unconsciousness of his approach, did not raise her
eyes from her book.

"Good - morning," said Tarrell, in a husky
voice.

Miss Boom returned the salutation, and, mark-
ing the place in her book with her forefinger,
looked over the hedge on the other side of the
road to the sea beyond.

"Your father has left his pouch behind, and
being as I was coming this way, asked me to
call for it," faltered the young man.

Miss Boom turned her head, and, regarding
him steadily, noted the rising colour and the
shuffling feet.

" Did he say where he had left it ? " she inquired.

" No," said the other.

" Well, my time's too valuable to waste looking
for pouches," said Kate, bending down to her
book again, " but if you like to go in and look
for it, you may ! "

She moved aside to let him pass, and sat listening with a slight smile as she heard him moving about the room.

"I can't find it," he said, after a pretended search.

"Better try the kitchen now then," said Miss Boom, without looking up, "and then the scullery. It might be in the woodshed or even down the garden. You haven't half looked."

She heard the kitchen door close behind him, and then, taking her book with her, went upstairs to her room. The conscientious Tarrell, having duly searched all the above-mentioned places, returned to the parlour and waited. He waited a quarter of an hour, and then going out by the front door, stood irresolute.

"I can't find it," he said at length, addressing himself to the bedroom window.

"No. I was coming down to tell you," said Miss Boom, glancing sedately at him from over the geraniums. "I remember seeing father take it out with him this morning."

Tarrell affected a clumsy surprise. "It doesn't matter," he said. "How nice your geraniums are."

"Yes, they're all right," said Miss Boom briefly.

"I can't think how you keep 'em so nice," said Tarrell.

"Well, don't try," said Miss Boom kindly.
"You'd better go back and tell father about
the pouch. Perhaps he's waiting for a smoke
all this time."

"There's no hurry," said the young man;
"perhaps he's found it."

"Well, I can't stop to talk," said the girl;
"I'm busy reading."

With these heartless words she withdrew into
the room, and the discomfited swain, only too
conscious of the sorry figure he cut, went slowly
back to the harbour, to be met by Mr. Boom
with a wink of aggravating and portentous
dimensions.

"You've took a long time," he said slyly.
"There's nothing like a little scheming in these
things."

"It didn't lead to much," said the discomfited
Tarrell.

"Don't be in a hurry, my lad," said the elder
man, after listening to his experiences. "I've
been thinking over this little affair for some
time now, an' I think I've got a plan."

"If it's anything about baccy pouches——"
began the young man ungratefully.

"It ain't," interrupted Mr. Boom, "it's quite
diff'rent. Now, you'd best get aboard your craft
and do your duty. There's more young men

won girls' 'arts while doing of their duty than—
than—if they wasn't doing their duty. Do you
understand me?"

It is inadvisable to quarrel with a prospective
father-in-law, so that Tarrell said he did, and
with a moody nod tumbled into his boat and
put off to the smack. Mr. Boom having walked
up and down a bit, and exchanged a few greet-
ings, bent his steps in the direction of the
"Jolly Sailor," and, ordering two mugs of ale,
set them down on a small bench opposite his
old friend Raggett.

"I see young Tarrell go off grumpy-like," said
Raggett, drawing a mug towards him and gazing
at the fast-receding boats.

"Ay, we'll have to do what we talked about,"
said Boom slowly. "It's opposition what that
gal wants. She simply sits and mopes for the
want of somebody to contradict her."

"Well, why don't you do it?" said Raggett.
"That ain't much for a father to do surely."

"I hev," said the other slowly, "more than
once. O' course, when I insist upon a thing, it's
done; but a woman's a delikit creeter, Raggett,
and the last row we had she got that ill that
she couldn't get up to get my breakfast ready,
no, nor my dinner either. It made us both ill,
that did."

"Are you going to tell Tarrell?" inquired Raggett.

"No," said his friend. "Like as not he'd tell her just to curry favour with her. I'm going to tell him he's not to come to the house no more. That'll make her want him to come, if anything will. Now there's no use wasting time. You begin to-day."

"I don't know what to say," murmured Raggett, nodding to him as he raised the beer to his lips.

"Just go now and call in—you might take her a nosegay."

"I won't do nothing so damned silly," said Raggett shortly.

"Well, go without 'em," said Boom impatiently; "just go and get yourselves talked about, that's all —have everybody making game of both of you, talking about a good-looking young girl being sweethearted by an old chap with one foot in the grave and a face like a dried herring. That's what I want."

Mr. Raggett, who was just about to drink, put his mug down again and regarded his friend fixedly.

"Might I ask who you're alloodin' to?" he inquired somewhat shortly.

Mr. Boom, brought up in mid-career, shuffled a little and laughed uneasily. "Them ain't my words, old chap," he said; "it was the way she was speaking of you the other day."

"Well, I won't have nothin' to do with it," said Raggett, rising.

"Well, nobody needn't know anything about it," said Boom, pulling him down to his seat again. "She won't tell, I'm sure—she wouldn't like the disgrace of it."

"Look here," said Raggett, getting up again.

"I mean from her point of view," said Mr. Boom querulously; "you're very 'asty, Raggett."

"Well, I don't care about it," said Raggett slowly; "it seemed all right when we was talking about it; but s'pose I have all my trouble for nothing, and she don't take Dick after all? What then?"

"Well, then there's no harm done," said his friend, "and it'll be a bit o' sport for both of us. You go up and start, an' I'll have another pint of beer and a clean pipe waiting for you against you come back."

Sorely against his better sense Mr. Raggett rose and went off, grumbling. It was fatiguing work on a hot day, climbing the road up the cliff, but he took it quietly, and having gained the top, moved slowly towards the cottage.

"Morning, Mr. Raggett," said Kate cheerily, as he entered the cottage. "Dear, dear, the idea of an old man like you climbing about! It's wonderful."

"I'm sixty-seven," said Mr. Raggett viciously, "and I feel as young as ever I did."

"To be sure," said Kate soothingly; "and look as young as ever you did. Come in and sit down a bit."

Mr. Raggett with some trepidation complied, and sitting in a very upright position, wondered how he should begin. "I am just sixty-seven," he said slowly. "I'm not old and I'm not young, but I'm just old enough to begin to want somebody to look after me a bit."

"I shouldn't while I could get about if I were you," said the innocent Kate. "Why not wait until you're bed-ridden?"

"I don't mean that at all," said Mr. Raggett snappishly. "I mean I'm thinking of getting married."

"Good—gracious!" said Kate, open-mouthed.

"I may have one foot in the grave, and resemble a dried herring in the face," pursued Mr. Raggett with bitter sarcasm, "but——"

"You can't help that," said Kate gently.

"But I'm going to get married," said Raggett savagely.

"Well, don't get in a way about it," said the girl. "Of course, if you want to, and—and—

you can find somebody else who wants to, there's no reason why you shouldn't! Have you told father about it?"

"I have," said Mr. Raggett, "and he has given his consent."

He put such meaning into this remark, and so much more in the contortion of visage which accompanied it, that the girl stood regarding him in blank astonishment.

"His consent?" she said in a strange voice.

Mr. Raggett nodded.

"I went to him first," he said, trying to speak confidently. "Now I've come to you—I want you to marry me!"

"Don't you be a silly old man, Mr. Raggett," said Kate, recovering her composure. "And as for my father, you go back and tell him I want to see him."

She drew aside and pointed to the door, and Mr. Raggett, thinking that he had done quite enough for one day, passed out and retraced his steps to the "Jolly Sailor." Mr. Boom met him half-way, and having received his message, spent the rest of the morning in fortifying himself for the reception which awaited him.

It would be difficult to say which of the two young people was the more astonished at this sudden change of affairs. Miss Boom, pretending to think that her parent's reason was affected, treated him accordingly, a state of affairs not without its drawbacks, as Mr. Boom found to his cost. Tarrell, on the other hand, attributed it to greed, and being forbidden the house, spent all his time ashore on a stile nearly opposite, sullenly watching events.

For three weeks Mr. Raggett called daily, and after staying to tea, usually wound up the evening by formally proposing for Kate's hand. Both conspirators were surprised and disappointed at the quietness with which Miss Boom received these attacks; Mr. Raggett meeting with a politeness which was a source of much wonder to both of them.

His courting came to an end suddenly. He paused one evening with his hand on the door, and having proposed in the usual manner, was going out, when Miss Boom called him back.

"Sit down, Mr. Raggett," she said calmly. Mr. Raggett, wondering inwardly, resumed his seat.

"You have asked me a good many times to marry you," said Kate.

"I have," said Mr. Raggett, nodding.

"And I'm sure it's very kind of you," continued the girl, "and if I've hurt your feelings by refusing you, it is only because I have thought perhaps I was not good enough for you."

In the silence which followed this unexpected and undeserved tribute to Mr. Raggett's worth, the two old men eyed each other in silent consternation.

" Still, if you 've made up your mind," continued the girl, " I don't know that it 's for me to object. You 're not much to look at, but you 've got the loveliest chest of drawers and the best furniture all round in Mastleigh. And I suppose you 've got a little money ? "

Mr. Raggett shook his head, and in a broken voice was understood to say: " A very little."

" I don't want any fuss or anything of that kind," said Miss Boom calmly. " No brides-maids or anything of that sort; it wouldn't be suitable at your age."

Mr. Raggett withdrew his pipe, and holding it an inch or two from his mouth, listened like one in a dream.

" Just a few old friends, and a bit of cake," continued Miss Boom musingly. " And instead of spending a lot of money in foolish waste, we 'll have three weeks in London."

Mr. Raggett made a gurgling noise in his throat, and suddenly remembering himself, pretended to think that it was something wrong with his pipe, and removing it blew noisily through the mouthpiece.

"Perhaps," he said, in a trembling voice—"perhaps you'd better take a little longer to consider, my dear."

Kate shook her head. "I've quite made up my mind," she said, "quite. And now I want to marry you just as much as you want to marry me. Good-night, father; good-night — George."

Mr. Raggett started violently, and collapsed in his chair.

"Raggett," said Mr. Boom huskily.

"Don't talk to me," said the other, "I can't bear it."

Mr. Boom, respecting his friend's trouble, relapsed into silence again, and for a long time not a word was spoken.

"My 'ed's in a whirl," said Mr. Raggett at length.

"It 'ud be a wonder if it wasn't," said Mr. Boom sympathetically.

"To think," continued the other miserably, "how I've been let in for this. The plots an' the plans and the artfulness what's been goin' on round me, an' I've never seen it."

"What d'ye mean?" demanded Mr. Boom, with sudden violence.

"I know what I mean," said Mr. Raggett darkly.

" P'raps you 'll tell me then," said the other.

"Who thought of it first?" demanded Mr. Raggett ferociously. "Who came to me and asked me to court his slip of a girl?"

"Don't you be a old fool," said Mr. Boom heatedly. "It's done now, and what's done can't be undone. I never thought to have a son-in-law seven or eight years older than what I am, and what's more, I don't want it."

"Said I wasn't much to look at, but she liked my chest o' drawers," repeated Raggett mechanically.

"Don't ask me where she gets her natur' from, cos I couldn't tell you," said the unhappy parent; "she don't get it from me."

Mr. Raggett allowed this reflection upon the late Mrs. Boom to pass unnoticed, and taking his hat from the table fixed it firmly upon his head, and gazing with scornful indignation upon his host, stepped slowly out of the door without going through the formality of bidding him good-night.

"George," said a voice from above him.

Mr. Raggett started, and glanced up at somebody leaning from the window.

"Come in to tea to-morrow early," said the voice pressingly; "good-night, dear."

Mr. Raggett turned and fled into the night, dimly conscious that a dark figure had detached itself from the stile opposite, and was walking beside him.

"That you, Dick?" he inquired nervously, after an oppressive silence.

"That's me," said Dick. "I heard her call you 'dear.'" Mr. Raggett, his face suffused with blushes, hung his head.

"Called you 'dear,'" repeated Dick; "I heard her say it. I'm going to pitch you in the harbour. I'll learn you to go courting a young girl. What are you stopping for?"

Mr. Raggett delicately intimated that he was stopping because he preferred, all things considered, to be alone. Finding the young man, however, bent upon accompanying him, he divulged the plot of which he had been the victim, and bitterly lamented his share in it.

"You don't want to marry her then?" said the astonished Dick.

"Course I don't," snarled Mr. Raggett; "I can't afford it. I'm too old; besides which, she'll turn my little place topsy-turvy. Look here, Dick, I done this all for you. Now, it's evident she only wants my furniture: if I give all the best of it to you, she'll take you instead."

"No, she won't," said Dick grimly; "I wouldn't have her now, not if she asked me on her bended knee."

"Why not?" said Raggett.

"I don't want to marry that sort o' girl," said the other scornfully; "it's cured me."

"What about me then?" said the unfortunate Raggett.

"Well, so far as I can see it serves you right for mixing in other people's business," said Dick shortly. "Well, good-night, and good luck to you."

To Mr. Raggett's sore disappointment he kept to his resolution, and being approached by Mr. Boom on his elderly friend's behalf, was rudely frank to him.

"I'm a free man again," he said blithely, "and I feel better than I've felt for ever so long. More manly."

"You ought to think of other people," said Mr. Boom severely; "think of poor old Raggett."

"Well, he's got a young wife out of it," said Dick. "I dare say he'll be happy enough. He wants somebody to help him spend his money."

In this happy frame of mind he resumed his ordinary life, and when he encountered his former idol, met her with a heartiness and unconcern which the lady regarded with secret disapproval. He was now so sure of himself that, despite a suspicion of ulterior design on the part of Mr. Boom, he even accepted an invitation to tea.

The presence of Mr. Raggett made it a slow and solemn function. Nobody with any feelings could eat with an appetite with that afflicted man at the table, and the meal passed almost in silence. Kate cleared the meal away, and the men sat at the open door with their pipes while she washed up in the kitchen.

"Me an' Raggett thought o' stepping down to the 'Sailor,'" said Mr. Boom, after a third application of his friend's elbow.

"I 'll come with you," said Dick.

"Well, we 've got a little business to talk about," said Boom confidentially; "but we sha'n't be long. If you wait here, Dick, we 'll see you when we come back."

"All right," said Tarrell.

He watched the two old men down the road, and then, moving his chair back into the room, silently regarded the busy Kate.

"Make yourself useful," said she brightly; "shake the tablecloth."

Tarrell took it to the door, and having shaken it, folded it with much gravity, and handed it back.

"Not so bad for a beginner," said Kate, taking it and putting it in a drawer. She took some needlework from another drawer, and, sitting down, began busily stitching.

" Wedding-dress ? " inquired Tarrell, with an assumption of great ease.

" No, tablecloth ! " said the girl, with a laugh. " You 'll want to know a little more before you get married."

" Plenty o' time for me," said Tarrell ; " I 'm in no hurry."

The girl put her work down and looked up at him.

" That 's right," she said staidly. " I suppose you were rather surprised to hear I was going to get married ? "

" A little," said Tarrell ; " there 's been so many after old Raggett, I didn't think he 'd ever be caught."

" Oh ! " said Kate.

" I dare say he 'll make a very good husband," said Tarrell patronisingly. " I think you 'll make a nice couple. He 's got a nice home."

" That 's why I 'm going to marry him," said Kate. " Do you think it 's wrong to marry a man for that ? "

" That 's your business," said Tarrell coldly. " Speaking for myself, and not wishing to hurt your feelings, *I* shouldn't like to marry a girl like that."

" You mean you wouldn't like to marry me ? " said Kate softly.

She leaned forward as she spoke, until her breath fanned his face.

"That's what I do mean," said Tarrell, with a suspicion of doggedness in his voice.

"Not even if I asked you on my bended knees?" said Kate. "Aren't you glad you're cured?"

"Yes," said Tarrell manfully.

"So am I," said the girl; "and now that you are happy, just go down to the 'Jolly Sailor,' and make poor old Raggett happy too."

"How?" asked Tarrell.

"Tell him that I have only been having a joke with him," said Kate, surveying him with a steady smile. "Tell him that I overheard him and father talking one night, and that I resolved to give them both a lesson. And tell them that I didn't think anybody could have been so stupid as they have been to believe in it."

She leaned back in her chair, and, regarding the dumbfounded Tarrell with a smile of wicked triumph, waited for him to speak. "Raggett, indeed!" she said disdainfully.

"I suppose," said Tarrell at length, speaking very slowly, "my being stupid was no surprise to you?"

"Not a bit," said the girl cheerfully.

"I'll ask you to tell Raggett yourself," said Tarrell, rising and moving towards the door. "I sha'n't see him. Good-night."

"Good-night," said she.   "Where are you going, then?"

There was no reply.

"Where are you going?" she repeated.   Then a suspicion of his purpose flashed across her. "You're not foolish enough to be going away?" she cried in dismay.

"Why not?" said Tarrell slowly.

"Because," said Kate, looking down—"oh, because—well, it's ridiculous.   I'd sooner have you stay here and feel what a stupid you've been making of yourself.   I want to remind you of it sometimes."

"I don't want reminding," said Tarrell, taking Raggett's chair; "I know it now."

A RASH EXPERIMENT

THE hands on the wharf had been working all Saturday night and well into the Sunday morning to finish the *Foam*, and now, at ten o'clock, with hatches down and freshly-scrubbed decks, the skipper and mate stood watching the tide as it rose slowly over the smooth Thames mud.

"What time's she coming?" inquired the skipper, turning a lazy eye up at the wharf.

"About ha'-past ten she said," replied the mate. "It's very good o' you to turn out and let her have your state-room."

"Don't say another word about that," said the skipper impressively. "I've met your wife once or twice, George, an' I must say that a nicer spoken woman, an' a more well-be'aved one, I've seldom seen."

"Same to you," said the mate; "your wife I mean."

"Any man," continued the skipper, "as would lay in a comfortable state-room, George, and leave a lady a-trying to turn and to dress and ondress herself in a poky little locker, ought to be ashamed of himself."

"You see, it's the luggage they bring," said the mate, slowly refilling his pipe. "What they want with it all I can't think. As soon as my old woman makes up her mind to come for a trip, to-morrow being Bank Holiday, an' she being in the mind for a outing, what does she do? Goes down Commercial Road and buys a bonnet far beyond her station."

"They're all like it," said the skipper; "mine's just as bad. What does that boy want?"

The boy approached the edge of the jetty, and, peering down at them, answered for himself.

"Who's Captain Bunnett?" he demanded shrilly.

"That's me, my lad," said the skipper, looking up.

"I've got a letter for yer," said the boy, holding it out.

The skipper held out his hands and caught it; and, after reading the contents, felt his beard and looked at the mate.

"It never rains but it pours," he said figuratively.

"What's up?" inquired the other.

"'Ere's my old woman coming now," said the skipper. "Sent a note to say she's getting ready as fast as she can, an' I'm not to sail on any account till she comes."

"That's awkward," said the mate, who felt that he was expected to say something.

"It never struck me to tell her your wife was coming," said the skipper. "Where we're to put 'em both I don't know. I s'pose it's quite certain your wife'll come?"

"Certain," said the mate.

"No chance of 'er changing 'er mind?" suggested the skipper, looking away from him.

"Not now she's got that bonnet," replied the mate. "I s'pose there's no chance of your wife changing hers?"

The skipper shook his head. "There's one thing," he said hopefully, "they'll be nice company for each other. They'll have to 'ave the stateroom between 'em. It's a good job my wife ain't as big as yours."

"We'll be able to play four 'anded wist sometimes," said the mate, as he followed the skipper below to see what further room could be made.

"Crowded, but jolly," said the other.

The two cabs drove up almost at the same moment while they were below, and Mrs. Bunnett's cabman had no sooner staggered on to the jetty with her luggage than Mrs. Fillson's arrived with hers. The two ladies, who were entire strangers, stood regarding each other curiously as they looked down at the bare deck of the *Foam*.

"*George!*" cried Mrs. Fillson, who was a fine woman, raising her voice almost to a scream in the effort to make herself heard above the winch of a neighbouring steamer.

It was unfortunate perhaps that both officers of the schooner bore the same highly-respectable Christian name.

"*George!*" cried Mrs. Bunnett, glancing indignantly at the other lady.

"*Ge-orge!*" cried Mrs. Fillson, returning her looks with interest.

"Hussy," said Mrs. Bunnett under her breath, but not very much under.

"GEORGE!"

There was no response.

"*George!*" cried both ladies together.

Still no response, and they made a louder effort.

There was yet another George on board, in the forecastle, and, in response to pushes from curious friends below, he came up, and regarded the fair duettists open-mouthed.

"What d'yer want?" he said at length sheepishly.

"Will you tell Captain Bunnett that his wife, Mrs. Bunnett, is here?" said that lady, a thin little woman with bright black eyes.

"Yes, mum," said the seaman, and was hurrying off when Mrs. Fillson called him back.

"Will you tell Mr. Fillson that his wife, Mrs. Fillson, is up here?" she said politely.

"All right, mum," said the other, and went below to communicate the pleasing tidings. Both husbands came up on deck hastily, and a glance served to show them how their wives stood.

"How do you do, Cap'n Bunnett," said Mrs. Fillson, with a fascinating smile.

"Good-morning, marm," said the skipper, trying to avoid his wife's eye; "that's my wife, Mrs. Bunnett."

"Good-morning, ma'am," said Mrs. Fillson, adjusting the new bonnet with the tips of her fingers.

"Good-morning to you," said Mrs. Bunnett in a cold voice, and patronising. "You have come to bring your husband some of his things, I suppose?"

"She's coming with us," said the skipper, in a hurry to have it over. "Wait half a moment, and I'll help you down."

He got up on to the side and helped them both to the deck, and, with a great attempt at cheery conversation, led the way below, where, in the midst of an impressive silence, he explained that the ladies would have to share the state-room between them.

"That's the only way out of it," said the mate, after waiting in vain for them to say something.

"It's a fairish size when you come to look at it," said the skipper, putting his head on one side to see whether the bunk looked larger that way.

"Pack three in there at a pinch," said the mate hardily.

Still the ladies said nothing, but there was a storm-signal hoisted in Mrs. Bunnett's cheek, which boded no good to her husband. There was room only for one trunk in the state-room, and by prompt generalship Mrs. Fillson got hers in first. Having seen it safe she went up on deck, for a look round.

"George," said Mrs. Bunnett fiercely, as soon as they were alone.

"Yes, my dear," said her husband.

"Pack that woman off home," said Mrs. Bunnett sharply.

"I couldn't do that," said the skipper firmly. "It's your own fault; you should have said you was coming."

"Oh, I know you didn't want me to come," said Mrs. Bunnett, the roses on her bonnet trembling. "The mate can think of a little pleasure for *his* wife, but I can stay at home and do your mending and keep the house clean. Oh, I know; don't tell me."

E

"Well, it's too late to alter it," said her husband. "I must get up above now; you'd better come too."

Mrs. Bunnett followed him on deck, and, getting as far from the mate's wife as possible, watched with a superior air of part ownership the movements of the seamen as they got under way. A favourable westerly breeze was blowing, and the canvas once set she stood by her husband as he pointed out the various objects of interest on the banks of the river.

They were still in the thick of the traffic at dinner-time, so that the skipper was able, to his secret relief, to send the mate below to do the honours of the table. He came up from it pale and scared, and, catching the skipper's eye, hunched his shoulders significantly.

"No words?" inquired the latter anxiously, in a half-whisper.

"Not exactly words," replied the mate. "What you might call snacks."

"I know," said the other with a groan.

"If you don't now," said the mate, "you will at tea-time. I'm not going to sit down there with them alone again. You needn't think it. If you was to ask me what I've been eating I couldn't tell you."

He moved off a bit as his table companions came up on deck, and the master of the *Foam* deciding

to take the bull by the horns, called both of them
to him, and pointed out the beauties of the various
passing craft. In the midst of his discourse his
wife moved off, leaving the unhappy man conversing alone with Mrs. Fillson, her face containing an
expression such as is seen in the prints of the very
best of martyrs as she watched them.

At tea-time the men sat in misery; Mrs. Bunnett
passed Mrs. Fillson her tea without looking at her,
an example which Mrs. Fillson followed in handing
her the cut bread and butter. When she took the
plate back it was empty, and Mrs. Bunnett, con-
vulsed with rage, was picking the slices out of her
lap.

"Oh, I *am* sorry," said Mrs. Fillson.

"You 're not, ma'am," said Mrs. Bunnett fiercely.
"You did it a purpose."

"There, there!" said both men feebly.

"Of course my husband 'll sit quite calm and see
me insulted," said Mrs. Bunnett, rising angrily from
her seat.

"And my husband 'll sit still drinking tea while
I 'm given the lie," said Mrs. Fillson, bending an
indignant look upon the mate.

"If you think I 'm going to share the state-room
with that woman, George, you 're mistaken," said
Mrs. Bunnett in a terrible voice. "I 'd sooner sleep
on a doorstep."

"And I'd sooner sleep on the scraper," said Mrs. Fillson, regarding her foe's scanty proportions.

"Very well, me an' the mate'll sleep there," said the skipper wearily. "You can have the mate's bunk and Mrs. Fillson can have the locker. You don't mind, George?"

"Oh, George don't mind," said Mrs. Bunnett mimickingly; "anything'll do for George. If you'd got the spirit of a man, you wouldn't let me be insulted like this."

"And if you'd got the spirit of a man," said Mrs. Fillson, turning on her husband, "you wouldn't let them talk to me like this. You never stick up for me."

She flounced up on deck where Mrs. Bunnett, after a vain attempt to finish her tea, shortly followed her. The two men continued their meal for some time in silence.

"We'll have to 'ave a quarrel just to oblige them, George," said the skipper at length, as he put down his cup. "Nothing else'll satisfy 'em."

"It couldn't be done," said the mate, reaching over and clapping him on the back.

"Just pretend, I mean," said the other.

"It couldn't be done proper," said the mate; "they'd see through it. We've sailed together five years now, an' never 'ad what I could call a really nasty word."

"Well, if you can think o' anything," said the skipper, "say so. This sort o' thing is worrying."

"See how we get on at breakfast," said the mate, as he lit his pipe. "If that's as bad as this, we'll have a bit of a row to please 'em."

Breakfast next morning was, if anything, worse, each lady directly inciting her lord to acts of open hostility. In this they were unsuccessful, but in the course of the morning the husbands arranged matters to their own satisfaction, and at the next meal the storm broke with violence.

"I don't wish to complain or hurt anybody's feelings," said the skipper, after a side-wink at the mate, "but if you could eat your wittles with a little less noise, George, I'd take it as a favour."

"Would you?" said the mate, as his wife stiffened suddenly in her seat. "Oh!"

Both belligerents, eyeing each other ferociously, tried hard to think of further insults.

"Like a pig," continued the skipper grumblingly.

The mate hesitated so long for a crushing rejoinder that his wife lost all patience and rose to her feet crimson with wrath.

How dare you talk to my husband like that?" she demanded fiercely. "George, come up on deck this instant!"

"I don't mind what he says," said the mate, who had only just begun his dinner.

"You come away at once," said his wife, pushing his plate from him.

The mate got up with a sigh, and, meeting the look of horror - stricken commiseration in his captain's eye, returned it with one of impotent rage.

"Use a larger knife, cap'n," he said savagely. "You'll swallow that little 'un one of these days."

The skipper, with the weapon in question gripped in his fist, turned round and stared at him in petrified amazement.

"If I wasn't the cap'n o' this ship, George," he said huskily, "an' bound to set a good example to the men, I'd whop you for them words."

"It's all for your good, Captain Bunnett," said Mrs. Fillson mincingly. "There was a poor old workhouse man I used to give a penny to sometimes, who would eat with his knife, and he choked himself with it."

"Ay, he did that, and he hadn't got a mouth half the size o' yours," said the mate warningly.

"Cap'n or no cap'n, crew or no crew," said the skipper in a suffocating voice, "I can't stand this. Come up on deck, George, and repeat them words."

Before the mate could accept the invitation, he was dragged back by his wife, while at the same time Mrs. Bunnett, with a frantic scream, threw her arms round her husband's neck, and dared him to move.

"You wait till I get you ashore, my lad," said the skipper threateningly.

"I 'll have to bring the ship home after I 've done with you," retorted the mate as he passed up on deck with his wife.

During the afternoon the couples exchanged not a word, though the two husbands exchanged glances of fiery import, and later on, their spouses being below, gradually drew near to each other. The mate, however, had been thinking, and as they came together met his foe with a pleasant smile.

"Bravo, old man," he said heartily.

"What d' yer mean?" demanded the skipper in gruff astonishment.

"I mean the way you pretended to row me," said the mate. "Splendid you did it. I tried to back you up, but lor! I wasn't in it with you."

"What, d' yer mean to say you didn't mean what you said?" inquired the other.

"Why, o' course," said the mate with an appearance of great surprise. "You didn't, did you?"

"No," said the skipper, swallowing something in his throat. "No, o' course not. But you did it well, too, George. Uncommon well, you did."

"Not half so well as you did," said the mate. "Well, I s'pose we 've got to keep it up now."

"I s'pose so," said the skipper; "but we mustn't keep it up on the same things, George. Swallerin' knives an' that sort o' thing, I mean."

"No, no," said the mate hastily.

"An' if you could get your missus to go home by train from Summercove, George, we might have a little peace and quietness," added the other.

"She'd never forgive me if I asked her," said the mate; "you'll have to order it, cap'n."

"I won't do that, George," said the skipper firmly. "I'd never treat a lady like that aboard my ship. I 'ope I know 'ow to behave myself if I do eat with my knife."

"Stow that," said the mate, reddening. "We'll wait an' see what turns up," he added hopefully.

For the next three days nothing fresh transpired, and the bickering between the couples, assumed on the part of the men and virulent on the part of their wives, went from bad to worse. It was evident that the ladies preferred it to any other amusement life on ship-board could offer, and, after a combined burst of hysterics on their part, in which the whole ship's company took a strong interest, the husbands met to discuss heroic remedies.

"It's getting worse and worse," said the skipper ruefully. "We'll be the laughing-stock o' the crew even afore they're done with us. There's another day afore we reach Summercove, there's five or six days there, an' at least five back again."

"There'll be murder afore then," said the mate, shaking his head.

"If we could only pack 'em *both* 'ome by train," continued the skipper.

"That's an expense," said the mate.

"It 'ud be worth it," said the other.

"An' they wouldn't do it," said the mate, "neither of 'em."

"I've seen women having rows afore," said the skipper, "but then they could get away from each other. It's being boxed up in this little craft as does the mischief."

"S'pose we pretend the ship's not seaworthy," said the mate.

"Then they'd stand by us," said the skipper, "closer than ever."

"I b'leeve they would," said the mate. "They'd go fast enough if we'd got a case o' small-pox or anything like that aboard, though."

The skipper grunted assent.

"It 'ud be worth trying," said the mate. "We've pretended to have a quarrel. Now just as we're going into port let one of the hands, the boy if you like, pretend he's sickening for small-pox."

"How's he going to do it?" inquired the skipper derisively.

"You leave it to me," replied the other. "I've got an idea how it's to be done."

Against his better judgment the skipper, after some demur, consented, and the following day, when the passengers were on deck gazing at the small port of Summercove as they slowly approached it, the cook came up excitedly and made a communication to the skipper.

"What?" cried the latter. "Nonsense."

"What's the matter?" demanded Mrs. Bunnett, turning round.

"Cook, here, has got it into his head that the boy's got the small-pox," said the skipper.

Both women gave a faint scream.

"Nonsense," said Mrs. Bunnett, with a pale face.

"Rubbish," said Mrs. Fillson, clasping her hands nervously.

"Very good, mum," said the cook calmly. "You know best, o' course, but I was on a barque once what got it aboard bad, and I think I *ought* to know it when I see it."

"Yes; and now you think everything's the small-pox," said Mrs. Bunnett uneasily.

"Very well, mum," said the cook, spreading out his hands. "Will you come down an' 'ave a *look* at 'im?"

"No," snapped Mrs. Bunnett, retreating a pace or two.

"Will you come down an' 'ave a look at 'im, sir," inquired the cook.

"You stay where you are, George," said Mrs. Bunnett shrilly, as her husband moved forward. "Go farther off, cook."

"And keep your tongue still when we get to port," said the mate. "Don't go blabbing it all over the place, mind, or we shan't get nobody to work us out."

"Ay, ay," said the cook, moving off. "I ain't afraid of it—I've given it to people, but I've never took it myself yet."

"I'm sure I wish I was off this dreadful ship," said Mrs. Fillson nervously. "Nothing but unpleasantness. How long before we get to Summercove, Cap'n Bunnett?"

"'Bout a hour an' a 'arf ought to do it," said the skipper.

Both ladies sighed anxiously, and, going as far aft as possible, gazed eagerly at the harbour as it opened out slowly before them.

"I shall go back by train," said Mrs. Bunnett. "It's a shame, having my holiday spoilt like this."

"It's one o' them things what can't be helped," said her husband piously.

"You'd better give me a little money," continued his wife. "I shall get lodgings in the town for a day or two, till I see how things are going."

"It 'ud be better for you to get straight back home," said the skipper.

"Nonsense," said his wife sharply. "Suppose you take it yourself, I should have to be here to see you were looked after. I'm sure Mrs. Fillson isn't going home."

Mrs. Fillson, holding out her hand to Mr. Fillson, said she was sure she wasn't.

"It 'ud be a load off our minds if you did go," said the mate, speaking for both.

"Well, we're not going for a day or two at any rate," said Mrs. Bunnett, glancing almost amiably at Mrs. Fillson.

In face of this declaration, and in view of the persistent demands of the ladies, both men, with a very ill grace furnished them with some money.

"Don't say a word about it ashore, mind," said the mate, avoiding his chief's indignant gaze.

"But you must have a doctor," said Mrs. Bunnett.

"I know of a doctor here," said the mate; "that's all arranged for."

He moved away for a little private talk with the skipper, but that gentleman was not in a conversational mood, and a sombre silence fell upon all until they were snugly berthed at Summercove, and the ladies, preceded by their luggage on a

trolly, went off to look for lodgings. They sent
down an hour later to say that they had found
them, and that they were very clean and comfortable, but a little more than they had intended to
give. They implored their husbands not to run
any unnecessary risks, and sent some disinfectant
soap for them to wash with.

For three days they kept their lodgings and
became fast friends, going, despite their anxiety,
for various trips in the neighbourhood. Twice a
day at least they sent down beef-tea and other
delicacies for the invalid, which never got farther
than the cabin, communication being kept up by
a small boy who had strict injunctions not to go
aboard. On the fourth day in the early morning
they came down as close to the ship as they dared
to bid farewell.

"Write if there's any change for the worse,"
cried Mrs. Bunnett.

"Or if you get it, George," cried Mrs. Fillson
anxiously.

"It's all right, he's going on beautiful," said the
mate.

The two wives appeared to be satisfied, and
with a final adieu went off to the railway station,
turning at every few yards to wave farewells until
they were out of sight.

"If ever I have another woman aboard my

ship, George," said the skipper, "I'll run into
something. Who's the old gentleman?"

He nodded in the direction of an elderly man
with white side-whiskers, who, with a black bag in
his hand, was making straight for the schooner.

"Captain Bunnett?" he inquired sharply.

"That's me, sir," said the skipper.

"Your wife sent me," said the tall man briskly.
"My name's Thompson—Dr. Thompson. She
says you've got a case of small-pox on board
which she wants me to see."

"We've got a doctor," said the skipper and
mate together.

"So your wife said, but she wished me particularly to see the case," said Dr. Thompson.
"It's also my duty as the medical officer of the
port."

"You've done it, George, you've done it,"
moaned the panic-stricken skipper reproachfully.

"Well, anybody can make a mistake," whispered
the mate back; "an' he can't touch us, as it *ain't*
small-pox. Let him come, and we'll lay it on to
the cook. Say he made a mistake."

"That's the ticket," said the skipper, and turned
to assist the doctor to the deck as the mate hurried
below to persuade the indignant boy to strip and
go to bed.

In the midst of a breathless silence the doctor

examined the patient; then, to the surprise of all, he turned to the crew and examined them one after the other.

"How long has this boy been ill?" he demanded.

"About four days," said the puzzled skipper.

"You see what comes of trying to hush this kind of thing up," said the doctor sternly. "You keep the patient down here instead of having him taken away and the ship disinfected, and now all these other poor fellows have got it."

"*What?*" screamed the skipper, as the crew broke into profane expressions of astonishment and self-pity. "Got what?"

"Why, the small-pox," said the doctor. "Got it in its worst form too. Suppressed. There's not one of them got a mark on him. It's all inside."

"Well, I'm damned," said the skipper, as the crew groaned despairingly.

"What else did you expect?" inquired the doctor wrathfully. "Well, they can't be moved now; they must all go to bed, and you and the mate must nurse them."

"And s'pose we catch it?" said the mate feelingly.

"You must take your chance," said the doctor; then he relented a little. "I'll try to send a couple of nurses down this afternoon," he added.

"In the meantime you must do what you can for them."

"Very good, sir," said the skipper brokenly.

"All you can do at present," said the doctor, as he slowly mounted the steps, "is to sponge them all over with cold water. Do it every half-hour till the rash comes out."

"Very good," said the skipper again. "But you'll hurry up with the nurses, sir!"

He stood in a state of bewilderment until the doctor was out of sight, and then, with a heavy sigh, took his coat off and set to work.

He and the mate, after warning off the men who had come down to work, spent all the morning in sponging their crew, waiting with an impatience born of fatigue for the rash to come out. This impatience was shared by the crew, the state of mind of the cook after the fifth sponging calling for severe rebuke on the part of the skipper.

"I wish the nurses 'ud come, George," he said, as they sat on the deck panting after their exertions; "this is a pretty mess if you like."

"Seems like a judgment," said the mate wearily.

"Halloa, there," came a voice from the quay.

Both men turned and looked up at the speaker.

"Halloa," said the skipper dully.

"What's all this about small-pox?" demanded the new-comer abruptly.

The skipper waved his hand languidly towards the forecastle.

"Five of 'em down with it," he said quietly. "Are you another doctor, sir?"

Without troubling to reply, their visitor jumped on board and went nimbly below, followed by the other two.

"Stand out of the light," he said brusquely. "Now, my lads, let's have a look at you."

He examined them in a state of bewilderment, grunting strangely as the washed-out men submitted to his scrutiny.

"They've had the best of cold sponging," said the skipper, not without a little pride.

"Best of what?" demanded the other.

The skipper told him, drawing back indignantly as the doctor suddenly sat down and burst into a hoarse roar of laughter. The unfeeling noise grated harshly on the sensitive ears of the sick men, and Joe Burrows, raising himself in his bunk, made a feeble attempt to hit him.

"You've been sold," said the doctor, wiping his eyes.

"I don't take your meaning," said the skipper with dignity.

"Somebody's been having a joke with you," said the doctor. "Get up, you fools; you've got about as much small-pox as I have."

F

"Do you mean to tell me——" began the skipper.

"Somebody's been having a joke with you, I tell you," repeated the doctor, as the men, with sundry oaths, half of relief, half of dudgeon, got out of bed and began groping for their clothes. "Who is it, do you think?"

The skipper shook his head, and the mate, following his lead, in duty bound, shook his; but a little while after, as they sat by the wheel smoking and waiting for the men to return to work the cargo out, they were more confidential. The skipper removed his pipe from his mouth, and, having eyed the mate for some time in silence, jerked his thumb in the direction of the railway station. The mate, with a woe-begone nod, assented.

THE CABIN PASSENGER

THE captain of the *Fearless* came on to the wharf in a manner more suggestive of deer-stalking than that of a prosaic shipmaster returning to his craft. He dodged round an empty van, lurked behind an empty barrel, flitted from that to a post, and finally from the interior of a steam crane peeped melodramatically on to the deck of his craft.

To the ordinary observer there was no cause for alarm. The decks were a bit slippery but not dangerous except to a novice; the hatches were on, and in the lighted galley the cook might be discovered moving about in a manner indicative of quiet security and an untroubled conscience.

With a last glance behind him the skipper descended from the crane and stepped lightly aboard.

"Hist," said the cook, coming out quietly. "I've been watching for you to come."

"Damned fine idea of watching you've got," said the skipper irritably. "What is it?"

The cook jerked his thumb towards the cabin. "He's down there," he said in a hoarse whisper. "The mate said when you came aboard you was just to go and stand near the companion and whistle 'God Save the Queen' and he'll come up to you to see what's to be done."

"*Whistle!*" said the skipper, trying to moisten his parched lips with his tongue. "I couldn't whistle just now to save my life."

"The mate don't know what to do, and that was to be the signal," said the cook. "He's darn there with him givin' 'im drink and amoosin' 'im."

"Well, you go and whistle it," said the skipper.

The cook wiped his mouth on the back of his hand. "'Ow does it go?" he inquired anxiously. "I never could remember toons."

"Oh, go and tell Bill to do it!" said the skipper impatiently.

Summoned noiselessly by the cook, Bill came up from the forecastle, and on learning what was required of him pursed up his lips and started our noble anthem with a whistle of such richness and volume that the horrified skipper was almost deafened with it. It acted on the mate like a charm, and he came from below and closed Bill's mouth, none too gently, with a hand which shook with excitement. Then, as quietly as possible, he closed the companion and secured the fasten-ings.

"He's all right," he said to the skipper breath-lessly. "He's a prisoner. He's 'ad four goes o' whisky, an' he seems inclinēd to sleep."

"Who let him go down the cabin?" demanded the skipper angrily. "It's a fine thing I can't leave the ship for an hour or so but what I come back and find people sitting all round my cabin."

"He let hisself darn," said the cook, who saw a slight opening advantageous to himself in con-nection with a dish smashed the day before, "an' I was that surprised, not to say alarmed, that I dropped the large dish and smashed it."

"What did he say?" inquired the skipper.

"The blue one, I mean," said the cook, who wanted that matter settled for good, "the one with the place at the end for the gravy to run into."

"What did he say?" vociferated the skipper.

"'E ses, ''Ullo,' he ses, 'you've done it now, old man,'" replied the truthful cook.

The skipper turned a furious face to the mate.

"When the cook come up and told me," said the mate, in answer, "I see at once what was up, so I went down and just talked to him clever like."

"I should like to know what you said," muttered the skipper.

"Well, if you think you can do better than I did you'd better go down and see him," retorted the mate hotly. "After all, it's you what 'e come to see. He's your visitor."

"No offence, Bob," said the skipper. "I didn't mean nothing."

"I don't know nothin' o' horse racin'," continued the mate, with an insufferable air, "and I never 'ad no money troubles in my life, bein' always brought up proper at 'ome and warned of what would 'appen, but I know a sheriff's officer when I see 'im."

"What am I to do?" groaned the skipper, too depressed even to resent his subordinate's manner. "It's a judgment summons. It's ruin if he gets me."

"Well, so far as I can see, the only thing for you to do is to miss the ship this trip," said the mate, without looking at him. "I can take her out all right."

"I won't," said the skipper, interrupting fiercely.

"Very well, you'll be nabbed" said the mate.

"You've been wanting to handle this craft a long time," said the skipper fiercely. "You could ha' got rid of him if you'd wanted to. He's no business down my cabin."

"I tried everything I could think of," asseverated the mate.

"Well, he's come down on my ship without being asked," said the skipper fiercely, "and, damme, he can stay there. Cast off."

"But," said the mate, "s'pose——"

"Cast off," repeated the skipper. "He's come on my ship, and I'll give him a trip free."

"And where are you and the mate to sleep?" inquired the cook, who was a man of pessimistic turn of mind, and given to forebodings.

"In your bunks," said the skipper brutally. "Cast off there."

The men obeyed, grinning, and the schooner was soon threading her way in the darkness down the river, the skipper listening somewhat nervously for the first intimation of his captive's awakening.

He listened in vain that night, for the prisoner made no sign, but at six o'clock in the morning, when the *Fearless*, coming within sight of the Nore, began to dance like a cork upon the waters, the mate reported hollow groans from the cabin.

"Let him groan," said the skipper briefly, "as holler as he likes."

"Well, I'll just go down and see how he is," said the mate.

"You stay where you are," said the skipper sharply.

"Well, but you ain't going to starve the man?"

"Nothing to do with me," said the skipper ferociously; "if a man likes to come down and stay in my cabin, that's his business. I'm not supposed to know he's there; and if I like to lock my cabin up and sleep in a foc'sle what's got more fleas in it than ten other foc'sles put together, and what smells worse than ten foc'sles rolled into one, that's my business."

"Yes, but I don't want to berth for'ard too," grumbled the other. " He can't touch me. I can go and sleep in my berth."

"You'll do what I wish, my lad," said the skipper.

"I'm the mate," said the other darkly.

"And I'm the master," said the other; "if the master of a ship can stay down the foc'sle, I'm sure a tuppeny-ha'penny mate can."

"The men don't like it," objected the mate.

"Damn the men," said the skipper politely, "and as to starving the chap, there's a water-bottle full o' water in my state-room, to say nothing of a jug, and a bag o' biscuits under the table."

The mate walked off whistling, and the skipper, by no means so easy in his mind as he pretended to be, began to consider ways and means out of

the difficulty which he foresaw must occur when
they reached port.

"What sort o' looking chap is he?" he inquired
of the cook.

"Big, strong-looking chap," was the reply.

"Look as though he'd make a fuss if I sent
you and Bill down below to gag him when we
get to the other end?" suggested the skipper.

The cook said that judging by appearances
"fuss" would be no word for it.

"I can't understand him keeping so quiet," said
the skipper; "that's what gets over me."

"He's biding 'is time, I expect," said the cook
comfortingly. "He's a 'ard looking customer,
'sides which he's likely sea-sick."

The day passed slowly, and as night approached
a sense of mystery and discomfort overhung the
vessel. The man at the wheel got nervous, and
flattered Bill into keeping him company by asking
him to spin him a yarn. He had good reason for
believing that he knew his comrade's stock of
stories by heart, but in the sequel it transpired
that there was one, of a prisoner turning into a
cat and getting out of the porthole and running
up helmsmen's backs, which he hadn't heard
before. And he told Bill in the most effective
language he could command that he never wanted
to hear it again.

The night passed and day broke, and still the mysterious passenger made no sign. The crew got in the habit of listening at the companion and peeping through the skylight; but the door of the state-room was closed, and the cabin itself as silent as the grave. The skipper went about with a troubled face, and that afternoon, unable to endure the suspense any longer, civilly asked the mate to go below and investigate.

"I'd rather not," said the mate, shrugging his shoulders.

"I'd sooner he served me and have done with it," said the skipper. "I get thinking all sorts of awful things."

"Well, why don't you go down yourself?" said the mate. "He'd serve you fast enough, I've no doubt."

"Well, it may be just his artfulness," said the skipper; "an' I don't want to humour him if he's all right. I'm askin' it as a favour, Bob."

"I'll go if the cook'll come," said the mate after a pause.

The cook hesitated.

"Go on, cook," said the skipper sharply; "don't keep the mate waiting, and, whatever you do, don't let him come up on deck."

The mate led the way to the companion, and, opening it quietly, led the way below, followed by the cook. There was a minute's awful suspense, and then a wild cry rang out below, and the couple came dashing madly up on deck again.

"What is it ?" inquired the pallid skipper.

The mate, leaning for support against the wheel, opened his mouth, but no words came; the cook, his hands straight by his side and his eyes glassy, made a picture from which the crew drew back in awe.

" What's—the—matter ? " said the skipper again.

Then the mate, regaining his composure by an effort, spoke.

" You needn't trouble to fasten the companion again," he said slowly.

The skipper's face changed from white to gray. " Why not ? " he asked in a trembling voice.

" He's dead," was the solemn reply.

" Nonsense," said the other, with quivering lips. " He's shamming or else fainting. Did you try to bring him round ? "

" I did not," said the mate. " I don't deceive you. I didn't stay down there to do no restoring, and I don't think you would either."

"Go down and see whether you can wake him, cook," said the skipper.

"Not me," said the cook with a mighty shudder.

Two of the hands went and peeped furtively

down through the skylight. The empty cabin
looked strangely quiet and drear, and the door of
the state-room stood ajar. There was nothing to
satisfy their curiosity, but they came back looking
as though they had seen a ghost.

"What's to be done?" said the skipper
helplessly.

"Nothing can be done," said the mate. "He's
beyond our aid."

"I wasn't thinking about *him*," said the skipper.

"Well, the best thing *you* can do when we get
to Plymouth is to bolt," said the mate. "We'll
hide it up as long as we can to give you a start.
It's a hanging matter."

The hapless master of the *Fearless* wiped his
clammy brow. "I can't think he's dead," he said
slowly. "Who'll come down with me to see?"

"You'd better leave it alone," said the mate
kindly, "it ain't pleasant, and besides that we can
all swear up to the present that you haven't
touched him or been near him.

"Who'll come down with me?" repeated the
skipper. "I believe it's a trick, and that he'll
start up and serve me, but I feel I must go."

He caught Bill's eye, and that worthy seaman,
after a short tussle with his nerves, shuffled after
him. The skipper, brushing aside the mate, who
sought to detain him, descended first, and entering

the cabin stood hesitating, with Bill close behind him.

"Just open the door, Bill," he said slowly.

"Arter you, sir," said the well-bred Bill.

The skipper stepped slowly towards it and flung it suddenly open. Then he drew back with a sharp cry and looked nervously about him. *The bed was empty.*

"Where's he gone?" whispered the trembling Bill.

The other made no reply, but in a dazed fashion began to grope about the cabin. It was a small place and soon searched, and the two men sat down and eyed each other in blank amazement.

"Where is he?" said Bill at length.

The skipper shook his head helplessly, and was about to ascribe the mystery to supernatural agencies when the truth in all its naked simplicity flashed upon him and he spoke. "It's the mate," he said slowly, "the mate and the cook. I see it all now; there's never been anybody here. It was a little job on the mate's part to get the ship. If you want to hear a couple o' rascals sized up, Bill, come on deck."

And Bill, grinning in anticipation, went.

THE day was fine, and the breeze so light
that the old patched sails were taking the
schooner along at a gentle three knots per hour.
A sail or two shone like snow in the offing, and
a gull hovered in the air astern. From the cabin
to the galley, and from the galley to the untidy
tangle in the bows, there was no sign of anybody
to benefit by the conversation of the skipper and
mate as they discussed a wicked and mutinous
spirit which had become observable in the crew.

"It's sheer rank wickedness, that's what it
is," said the skipper, a small elderly man, with
grizzled beard and light blue eyes.

"Rank," agreed the mate, whose temperament
was laconic.

"Why, when I was a boy you wouldn't believe
what I had to eat," said the skipper; "not if I
took my Bible oath on it, you wouldn't."

"They're dainty," said the mate.

"Dainty!" said the other indignantly. "What
right have hungry sailormen to be dainty? Don't

I give them enough to eat? Look! Look there!"

He drew back, choking, and pointed with his forefinger as Bill Smith, A.B., came on deck with a plate held at arm's length, and a nose disdainfully elevated. He affected not to see the skipper, and, walking in a mincing fashion to the side, raked the food from the plate into the sea with his fingers. He was followed by George Simpson, A.B., who in the same objectionable fashion wasted food which the skipper had intended should nourish his frame.

"I'll pay 'em for this!" murmured the skipper.

"There's some more," said the mate.

Two more men came on deck, grinning consciously, and disposed of their dinners. Then there was an interval — an interval in which everybody, fore and aft, appeared to be waiting for something; the something being at that precise moment standing at the foot of the foc'sle ladder, trying to screw its courage up.

"If the boy comes," said the skipper in a strained, unnatural voice, "I'll flay him alive."

"You'd better get your knife out then," said the mate.

The boy appeared on deck, very white about the gills, and looking piteously at the crew for support. He became conscious from their scowls that he had forgotten something, and remembering himself, stretched out his skinny arms to their full extent, and, crinkling his nose, walked with great trepidation to the side.

"Boy!" vociferated the skipper suddenly.

"Yessir," said the urchin hastily.

"Comm'ere," said the skipper sternly.

"Shove your dinner over first," said four low, menacing voices.

The boy hesitated, then walked slowly towards the skipper.

"What are you going to do with that dinner?" demanded the latter grimly.

"Eat it," said the youth modestly.

"What d'yer bring it on deck for, then?' inquired the other, bending his brows on him.

"I thought it would taste better on deck, sir," said the boy.

"Taste better!" growled the skipper ferociously. "Ain't it good?"

"Yessir," said the boy.

"Speak louder," said the skipper sternly. "Is it very good?"

"Beautiful," said the boy in a shrill falsetto.

"Did you ever taste better wittles than you get aboard this ship?" demanded the skipper, setting him a fine example in loud speaking.

"Never," yelled the boy, following it.

"Everything as it should be?" roared the skipper.

"Better than it should be," shrilled the craven.

"Sit down and eat it," commanded the other.

The boy sat on the cabin skylight, and, taking out his pocket-knife, began his meal with every appearance of enjoyment, the skipper, with his elbows on the side, and his legs crossed, regarding him serenely.

"I suppose," he said loudly, after watching the boy for some time, "I s'pose the men threw theirs overboard becos they hadn't been used to such good food?"

"Yessir," said the boy.

"Did they say so?" bawled the other.

The boy hesitated, and glanced nervously forward. "Yessir," he said at length, and shuddered as a low, ominous growl came from the crew. Despite his slowness, the meal came to an end at last, and, in obedience to orders, he rose, and taking his plate forward, looked entreatingly at the crew as he passed them.

"Come down below," said Bill; "we want to have a talk with you."

"Can't," said the boy. "I've got my work to do. I haven't got time to talk."

He stayed up on deck until evening, and then, the men's anger having evaporated somewhat,

G

crept softly below, and climbed into his bunk. Simpson leaned over and made a clutch at him, but Bill pushed him aside.

"Leave him alone," said he quietly; "we'll take it out of him to-morrow."

For some time Tommy lay worrying over the fate in store for him, and then, yielding to fatigue, turned over and slept soundly until he was awakened some three hours later by the men's voices, and, looking out, saw that the lamp was alight and the crew at supper, listening quietly to Bill, who was speaking.

"I've a good mind to strike, that's what I've a good mind to do," he said savagely, as, after an attempt at the butter, he put it aside and ate dry biscuit.

"An' get six months," said old Ned. "That won't do, Bill."

"Are we to go a matter of six or seven days on dry biscuit and rotten taters?" demanded the other fiercely. "Why, it's slow sooicide."

"I wish one of you would commit sooicide," said Ned, looking wistfully round at the faces, "that 'ud frighten the old man, and bring him round a bit."

"Well, you're the eldest," said Bill pointedly.

"Drowning's a easy death too," said Simpson persuasively. "You can't have much enjoyment in life at your age, Ned?"

"And you might leave a letter behind to the skipper, saying as 'ow you was drove to it by bad food," said the cook, who was getting excited.

"Talk sense!" said the old man very shortly.

"Look here," said Bill suddenly. "I tell you what we can do : let one of us pretend to commit suicide, and write a letter as Slushy here ses, saying as 'ow we're gone overboard sooner than be starved to death. It 'ud scare the old man proper; and p'raps he'd let us start on the other meat without eating up this rotten stuff first."

"How's it to be done?" asked Simpson, staring.

"Go an' 'ide down the fore 'old," said Bill. "There's not much stuff down there. We'll take off the hatch when one of us is on watch to-night, and—whoever wants to—can go and hide down there till the old man's come to his senses. What do you think of it, mates?"

"It's all right as an idea," said Ned slowly, "but who's going?"

"Tommy," replied Bill simply.

"Blest if I ever thought of him," said Ned admiringly; "did you, cookie?"

"Never crossed my mind," said the cook.

"You see the best o' Tommy's going," said Bill, "is that the old man 'ud only give him a flogging if he found it out. We wouldn't split as to who put the hatch on over him. He can be there as comfortable as you please, do nothing, and sleep all day if he likes. O' course we don't know anything about it, we miss Tommy, and find the letter wrote on this table."

The cook leaned forward and regarded his colleague favourably; then he pursed his lips, and nodded significantly at an upper bunk from which the face of Tommy, pale and scared, looked anxiously down.

"Halloa!" said Bill, "have you heard what we've been saying?"

"I heard you say something about going to drown old Ned," said Tommy guardedly.

"He's heard all about it," said the cook severely. "Do you know where little boys who tell lies go to, Tommy?"

"I'd sooner go there than down the fore 'old," said Tommy, beginning to knuckle his eyes. "I won't go. I'll tell the skipper."

"No you won't," said Bill sternly. "This is your punishment for them lies you told about us to-day, an' very cheap you've got off too. Now, get out o' that bunk. Come on afore I pull you out."

With a miserable whimper the youth dived beneath his blankets, and, clinging frantically to the edge of his berth, kicked convulsively as he was lifted down, blankets and all, and accommodated with a seat at the table.

"Pen and ink and paper, Ned," said Bill.

The old man produced them, and Bill, first wiping off with his coat-sleeve a piece of butter which the paper had obtained from the table, spread it before the victim.

"I can't write," said Tommy sullenly.

The men looked at each other in dismay.

"It's a lie," said the cook.

"I tell you I can't," said the urchin, becoming hopeful; "that's why they sent me to sea, becos I couldn't read or write."

"Pull his ear, Bill," said Ned, annoyed at these aspersions upon an honourable profession.

"It don't matter," said Bill calmly. "I'll write it for 'im; the old man don't know my fist."

He sat down at the table, and, squaring his shoulders, took a noisy dip of ink, and scratching his head, looked pensively at the paper.

"Better spell it bad, Bill, suggested Ned.

"Ay, ay," said the other. "'Ow do you think a boy would spell 'sooicide,' Ned?"

The old man pondered. "S-o-o-e-y-s-i-d-e," he said slowly.

"Why, that's the right way, ain't it?" inquired the cook, looking from one to the other.

"We mustn't spell it right," said Bill, with

his pen hovering over the paper. "Be careful, Ned."

"We'll say 'killed myself' instead," said the old man. "A boy wouldn't use such a big word as that p'raps."

Bill bent over his work, and, apparently paying great attention to his friends' entreaties not to write it too well, slowly wrote the letter.

"How's this?" he inquired, sitting back in his seat.

"'Deer captin i take my pen in hand for the larst time to innform you that i am no more suner than heat the 'orrible stuff what you kall meet i have drownded miself it is a moor easy death than starvin' i 'ave left my clasp nife to bill an' my silver wotch to it is 'ard too dee so young tommie brown.'"

"Splendid!" said Ned, as the reader finished and looked inquiringly round.

"I put in that bit about the knife and the watch to make it seem real," said Bill, with modest pride; "but, if you like, I'll leave 'em to you instead, Ned."

"I don't want 'em," said the old man generously.

"Put your cloes on," said Bill, turning to the whimpering Tommy.

"I'm *not* going down that fore 'old," said

Tommy desperately. "You may as well know now as later on—I won't go."

"Cookie," said Bill calmly, "just 'and me them cloes, will you? Now, Tommy."

"I tell you I'm not going to," said Tommy.

"An' that little bit o' rope, cookie," said Bill; "it's just down by your 'and. Now, Tommy."

The youngest member of the crew looked from his clothes to the rope, and from the rope back to his clothes again.

"How'm I goin' to be fed?" he demanded sullenly, as he began to dress.

"You'll have a stone bottle o' water to take down with you an' some biskits," replied Bill, "an' of a night-time we'll hand you down some o' that meat you're so fond of. Hide 'em behind the cargo, an' if you hear anybody take the hatch off in the day-time, nip behind it yourself."

"An' what about fresh air?" demanded the sacrifice.

"You'll 'ave fresh air of a night when the hatch is took off," said Bill. "Don't you worry, I've thought of everything.

The arrangements being concluded, they waited until Simpson relieved the mate at the helm, and then trooped up on deck, half pushing and half leading their reluctant victim.

"It's just as if he was going on a picnic,"

said old Ned, as the boy stood unwillingly on the deck, with a stone bottle in one hand and some biscuits wrapped up in an old newspaper in the other.

"Lend a 'and, Bill. Easy does it."

Noiselessly the two seamen took off the hatch, and, as Tommy declined to help in the proceedings at all, Ned clambered down first to receive him. Bill took him by the scruff of the neck and lowered him, kicking strongly, into the hold.

"Have you got him?" he inquired.

"Yes," said Ned in a smothered voice, and, depositing the boy in the hold, hastily clambered up again, wiping his mouth.

"Been having a swig at the bottle?" inquired Bill.

"Boy's heel," said Ned very shortly. "Get the hatch on."

The hatch was replaced, and Bill and his fellow conspirator, treading quietly and not without some apprehension for the morrow, went below and turned in. Tommy, who had been at sea long enough to take things as he found them, curled up in the corner of the hold, and with his bottle as a pillow fell asleep.

It was not until eight o'clock next morning that the master of the *Sunbeam* discovered that he was a boy short. He questioned the cook as he sat at breakfast. The cook, who was a very nervous man, turned pale, set the coffee-pot down with a thump which upset some of the liquor, and bolted up on deck. The skipper, after shouting for him in some of the most alluring swear words known on the high seas, went raging up on deck, where he found the men standing in a little knot, looking very ill at ease.

"Bill," said the skipper uneasily, "what's the matter with that damned cook?"

"'E's 'ad a shock, sir," said Bill, shaking his head; "we've all 'ad a shock."

"You'll have another in a minute," said the skipper emotionally. "Where's the boy?"

For a moment Bill's hardihood forsook him, and he looked helplessly at his mates. In their anxiety to avoid his gaze they looked over the side, and a horrible fear came over the skipper. He looked at Bill mutely, and Bill held out a dirty piece of paper.

The skipper read it through in a state of stupefaction, then he handed it to the mate, who had followed him on deck. The mate read it and handed it back.

"It's yours," he said shortly.

"I don't understand it," said the skipper, shaking his head. "Why, only yesterday he was up on deck here eating his dinner, and saying it was the best meat he ever tasted. You heard him, Bob?"

"I *heard* him, pore little devil!" said the mate.

"You all heard him," said the skipper. "Well, there's five witnesses I've got. He must have been mad. Didn't nobody hear him go overboard?"

"I 'eard a splash, sir, in my watch," said Bill.

"Why didn't you run and see what it was?" demanded the other.

"I thought it was one of the chaps come up to throw his supper overboard," said Bill simply.

"Ah!" said the skipper, biting his lip, "did you? You're always going on about the grub. What's the matter with it?"

"It's pizon, sir," said Ned, shaking his head. "The meat's awful."

"It's as sweet as nuts," said the skipper. "Well, you can have it out of the other tank if you like. Will that satisfy you?"

The men brightened up a little and nudged each other.

"The butter's bad too, sir," said Bill.

"Butter bad!" said the skipper, frowning. "How's that, cook?"

"I ain't done nothing to it, sir," said the cook helplessly.

"Give 'em butter out o' the firkin in the cabin," growled the skipper. "It's my firm belief you'd been ill-using that boy; the food was delicious."

He walked off, taking the letter with him, and, propping it up against the sugar-basin, made but a poor breakfast.

For that day the men lived, as Ned put it, on the fat of the land, in addition to the other luxuries figgy duff, a luxury hitherto reserved for Sundays, being also served out to them. Bill was regarded as a big-brained benefactor of the human race; joy reigned in the foc'sle, and at night the hatch was taken off and the prisoner regaled with a portion which had been saved for him. He ate it ungratefully, and put churlish and inconvenient questions as to what was to happen at the end of the voyage.

"We'll smuggle you ashore all right," said Bill; "none of us are going to sign back in this old tub. I'll take you aboard some ship with me—Eh?"

"I didn't say anything," said Tommy untruthfully.

To the wrath and confusion of the crew, next day their commanding officer put them back on the old diet again. The old meat was again served out, and the grass-fed luxury from the cabin stopped. Bill shared the fate of all leaders when things go wrong, and, from being the idol of his fellows, became a butt for their gibes.

"What about your little idea now?" grunted old Ned, scornfully, that evening as he broke his biscuit roughly with his teeth, and dropped it into his basin of tea.

"You ain't as clever as you thought you was, Bill," said the cook with the air of a discoverer.

"And there's that pore dear boy shut up in the dark for nothing," said Simpson, with some-what belated thoughtfulness. "An' cookie doing his work."

"I'm not going to be beat," said Bill blackly; "the old man was badly scared yesterday. We must have another sooicide, that's all."

"Let Tommy do it again," suggested the cook flippantly, and they all laughed.

"Two on one trip'll about do the old man up," said Bill, regarding the interruption un-favourably. "Now, who's going to be the next?"

"We've had enough o' this game," said Simpson, shrugging his shoulders; "you've gone cranky, Bill."

"No I ain't," said Bill; "I'm not going to be beat, that's all. Whoever goes down, they'll have a nice, easy, lazy time. Sleep all day if he likes, and nothing to do. *You* ain't been looking very well lately, Ned."

"Oh?" said the old man coldly.

"Well, settle it between you," said Bill carelessly; "it's all one to me, which of you goes."

"Ho, an' what about you?" demanded Simpson.

"Me?" inquired Bill in astonishment. "Why, I've got to stay up here and manage it."

"Well, we'll stay up and help you," said Simpson derisively.

Ned and the cook laughed, Simpson joined in. Bill rose, and, going to his bunk, fished out a pack of greasy cards from beneath his bedding.

"Larst cut, sooicide," he said briefly. "I'm in it."

He held the pack before the cook. The cook hesitated, and looked at the other two.

"Don't be a fool, Bill," said Simpson.

"Why, do you funk it?" sneered Bill.

"It's a fool's game, I tell you," said Simpson.

"Well, you 'elped me start it," said the other. "You're afraid, that's what you are, afraid. You can let the boy go down there, but when it comes to yourselves you turn chicken-'arted."

"All right," said Simpson recklessly, "let Bill 'ave 'is way; cut, cookie."

Sorely against his will the cook complied, and drew a ten; Ned, after much argument, cut and drew seven; Simpson, with a king in his fist, leaned back on the locker and fingered his beard nonchalantly. "Go on, Bill," he said; "see what you can do."

Bill took the pack and shuffled it. "I orter be able to beat seven," he said slowly. He handed the pack to Ned, drew a card, and the other three sat back and laughed boisterously.

"Three!" said Simpson. "Bravo, Bill! I'll write your letter for you; he'd know your writing. What shall I say?"

"Say what you like," retorted Bill, breathing hard as he thought of the hold.

He sat back sneering disdainfully, as the other three merrily sat down to compose his letter, replying only by a contemptuous silence when Simpson asked him whether he wanted any kisses put in. When the letter was handed over for his inspection he only made one remark.

"I thought you could write better than that, George," he said haughtily.

"I'm writing it for you," said Simpson.

Bill's hauteur vanished and he became his old self again. "If you want a plug in the eye, George," he said feelingly, "you've only got to say so, you know."

His temper was so unpleasant that half the
pleasure of the evening was spoiled, and instead
of being conducted to his hiding-place with quips
and light laughter, the proceedings were more
like a funeral than anything else. The crowning
touch to his ill-nature was furnished by Tommy,
who upon coming up and learning that Bill was
to be his room-mate, gave way to a fit of the
most unfeigned horror.

"There's another letter for you this morning,"
said the mate, as the skipper came out of his
state-room buttoning up his waistcoat.

"Another what?" demanded the other, turning
pale.

The mate jerked his thumb upwards. "Old
Ned has got it," he continued. "I can't think
what's come over the men."

The skipper dashed up on deck, and mechanically took the letter from Ned and read it
through. He stood for some time like a man in
a dream, and then stumbled down the forecastle,
and looked in all the bunks and even under
the table; then he came up and stood by the
hold, with his head on one side. The men held
their breath.

"What's the meaning of all this?" he demanded
at length, sitting limply on the hatch, with his
eyes down.

"Bad grub, sir," said Simpson, gaining courage from his manner; "that's what we'll have to say when we get ashore."

"You're not to say a word about it!" said the other, firing up.

"It's our dooty, sir," said Ned impressively.

"Look here now," said the skipper, and he looked at the remaining members of the crew entreatingly. "Don't let's have no more suicides. The old meat's gone now, and you can start the other, and when we get to port I'll ship in some fresh butter and vegetables. But I don't want you to say anything about the food being bad, or about these letters, when we get to port. I shall simply say the two of 'em disappeared, an' I want you to say the same."

"It can't be done, sir," said Simpson firmly.

The skipper rose and walked to the side. "Would a fi'pun note make any difference?" he asked in a low voice.

"It 'ud make a little difference," said Ned cautiously.

The skipper looked up at Simpson. On the face of Simpson was an expression of virtuous arithmetical determination.

The skipper looked down again. "Or a fi'pun note each?" he said, in a low voice. "I can't go beyond that."

"Call it twenty pun and it's a bargain, ain't it, mates?" said Simpson.

Ned said it was, and even the cook forgot his nervousness, and said it was evident the skipper meant to do the generous thing, and they'd stand by him.

"Where's the money coming from?" inquired the mate, as the skipper went down to breakfast, and discussed the matter with him. "They wouldn't get nothing out of me!"

The skylight was open; the skipper with a glance at it bent forward and whispered in his ear.

"Wot!" said the mate. He endeavoured to suppress his laughter with hot coffee and bacon, with the result that he had to rise from his seat and stand patiently while the skipper dealt him some hearty thumps on the back.

With the prospect of riches before them the men cheerfully faced the extra work; the cook did the boy's, while Ned and Simpson did Bill's between them. When night came they removed the hatch again, and with a little curiosity waited to hear how their victims were progressing.

"Where's my dinner?" growled Bill hungrily, as he drew himself up on deck.

"Dinner!" said Ned, in surprise; "why, you ain't got none."

H

" *Wot ?* " said Bill ferociously.

"You see the skipper only serves out for three now," said the cook.

" Well, why didn't you save us some ? " demanded the other.

"There ain't enough of it, Bill, there ain't indeed," said Ned. "We have to do more work now, and there ain't enough even for us. You've got biscuit and water, haven't you ? "

Bill swore at him.

" I've 'ad enough o' this," he said fiercely. " I'm coming up, let the old man do what he likes. I don't care."

"Don't do that, Bill," said the old man persuasively. "Everything's going beautiful. You was quite right what you said about the old man. We was wrong. He's skeered fearful, and he's going to give us twenty pun to say nothing about it when we get ashore."

" I'm going to have ten out o' that," said Bill, brightening a little, "and it's worth it too. I get the 'orrors shut up down there all day."

"Ay, ay," said Ned, with a side kick at the cook, who was about to question Bill's method of division.

"The old man sucked it all in beautiful," said the cook. "He's in a dreadful way. He's got all your clothes and things, and the boy's, and he's going to 'and 'em over to your friends. It's the best joke I ever heard."

"You're a fool!" said Bill shortly, and lighting his pipe went and squatted in the bows to wrestle grimly with a naturally bad temper.

For the ensuing four days things went on smoothly enough. The weather being fair, the watch at night was kept by the men, and regularly they had to go through the unpleasant Jack-in-the-box experience of taking the lid off Bill. The sudden way he used to pop out and rate them about his sufferings and their callousness was extremely trying, and it was only by much persuasion and reminders of his share of the hush-money that they could persuade him to return again to his lair at daybreak.

Still undisturbed they rounded the Land's End. The day had been close and muggy, but towards night the wind freshened, and the schooner began to slip at a good pace through the water. The two prisoners, glad to escape from the stifling atmosphere of the hold, sat in the bows with an appetite which the air made only too keen for the preparations made to satisfy it.

Ned was steering, and the other two men having gone below and turned in, there were no listeners to their low complaints about the food.

"It's a fool's game, Tommy," said Bill, shaking his head.

"*Game?*" said Tommy, sniffing. "'Ow are we going to get away when we get to Northsea?"

"You leave that to me," said Bill. "Old Ned seems to ha' got a bad cough," he added.

"He's choking, I should think," said Tommy, leaning forward. "Look! he's waving his hand at us."

Both sprang up hastily, but ere they could make any attempt to escape the skipper and mate emerged from the companion and walked towards them.

"Look here," said the skipper, turning to the mate, and indicating the culprits with his hand; "perhaps you'll disbelieve in dreams now."

"'Strordinary!" said the mate, rubbing his eyes, as Bill stood sullenly waiting events, while the miserable Tommy skulked behind him.

"I've *heard* o' such things," continued the skipper, in impressive tones, "but I never expected to see it. You can't say you haven't seen a ghost now, Bob."

"'Strordinary!" said the mate, shaking his head again. "Lifelike!"

"The ship's haunted, Ned," cried the skipper in hollow tones. "Here's the sperrits o' Bill and the boy standing agin the windlass."

The bewildered old seaman made no reply; the smaller spirit sniffed and wiped his nose on his cuff, and the larger one began to whistle softly.

"Poor things!" said the skipper, after they had discussed these extraordinary apparitions for some time. "Can you see the windlass through the boy, Bob?"

"I can see through both of 'em," said the mate slyly.

They stayed on deck a little longer, and then coming to the conclusion that their presence on deck could do no good, and indeed seemed only to embarrass their visitors, went below again, leaving all hands a prey to the wildest astonishment.

"Wot's 'is little game?" asked Simpson, coming cautiously up on deck.

"Damned if I know," said Bill savagely.

"He don't really think you're ghosts?" suggested the cook feebly.

"O' course not," said Bill scornfully. "He's got some little game on. Well, I'm going to my bunk. You'd better come too, Tommy. We'll find out what it all means to-morrer, I've no doubt."

On the morrow they received a little enlightenment, for after breakfast the cook came forward

nervously to break the news that meat and vegetables had only been served out for three. Consternation fell upon all.

"I'll go an' see 'im," said Bill ravenously.

He found the skipper laughing heartily over
something with the mate. At the seaman's
approach he stepped back and eyed him
coolly.

"Mornin', sir," said Bill, shuffling up. "We'd
like to know, sir, me an' Tommy, whether we can
have our rations for dinner served out now same as
before?"

"*Dinner?*" said the skipper in surprise. "What
do you want dinner for?"

"Eat," said Bill, eyeing him reproachfully.

"Eat?" said the skipper. "What's the good o'
giving dinner to a ghost? Why you've got nowhere to put it."

By dint of great self-control Bill smiled in a
ghastly fashion, and patted his stomach.

"All air," said the skipper turning away.

"Can we have our clothes and things then?"
said Bill grinding his teeth. "Ned says as how
you've got 'em."

"Certainly not," said the skipper. "I take 'em
home and give 'em to your next o' kin. That's
the law, ain't it, Bob?"

"It is," said the mate.

"They'll 'ave your effects and your pay up to the night you committed suicide," said the skipper.

"We didn't commit sooicide," said Bill; "how could we when we're standing here?"

"Oh, yes, you did," said the other. "I've got your letters in my pocket to prove it; besides, if you didn't I should give you in charge for desertion directly we get to port."

He exchanged glances with the mate, and Bill, after standing first on one leg and then on the other, walked slowly away. For the rest of the morning he stayed below setting the smaller ghost a bad example in the way of language, and threatening his fellows with all sorts of fearful punishments.

Until dinner-time the skipper heard no more of them, but he had just finished that meal and lit his pipe when he heard footsteps on the deck, and the next moment old Ned, hot and angry, burst into the cabin.

"Bill's stole our dinner, sir," he panted unceremoniously.

"Who?" inquired the skipper coldly.

"Bill, sir, Bill Smith," replied Ned.

"*Who?*" inquired the skipper more coldly than before.

"The ghost o' Bill Smith," growled Ned, correcting himself savagely, "has took our dinner away, an' him an' the ghost o' Tommy Brown is a sitting down and boltin' of it as fast as they can bolt."

"Well, I don't see what I can do," said the skipper lazily. "What'd you let 'em for?"

"You know what Bill is, sir," said Ned. "I'm an old man, cook's no good, and unless Simpson has a bit o' raw beef for his eyes, he won't be able to see for a week."

"Rubbish!" said the skipper jocularly. "Don't tell me, three men all afraid o' one ghost. I shan't interfere. Don't you know what to do?"

"No, sir," said Ned eagerly.

"Go up and read the Prayer-book to him, and he'll vanish in a cloud of smoke," said the skipper.

Ned gazed at him for a moment speechlessly, and then going up on deck leaned over the side and swore himself faint. The cook and Simpson came up and listened respectfully, contenting themselves with an occasional suggestion when the old man's memory momentarily failed him.

For the rest of the voyage the two culprits suffered all the inconvenience peculiar to a loss of citizenship. The skipper blandly ignored them, and on two or three occasions gave great offence by attempting to walk through Bill as he stood on the deck. Speculation was rife in the forecastle as to what would happen when they got ashore,

and it was not until Northsea was sighted that
the skipper showed his hand. Then he appeared
on deck with their effects done up neatly in two
bundles, and pitched them on the hatches. The
crew stood and eyed him expectantly.

"Ned," said the skipper sharply.

"Sir," said the old man.

"As soon as we're made fast," said the other,
"I want you to go ashore for me and fetch an
undertaker and a policeman. I can't quite make
up my mind which I want."

"Ay, ay, sir," murmured the old man.

The skipper turned away, and seizing the helm
from the mate took his ship in. He was so intent
upon this business that he appeared not to notice
the movements of Bill and Tommy as they edged
nervously towards their bundles, and waited
impatiently for the schooner to get alongside
the quay. Then he turned to the mate and
burst into a loud laugh as the couple, bending
suddenly, snatched up their bundles, and, clamber-
ing up the side, sprang ashore and took to
their heels. The mate laughed too, and a faint
but mirthless echo came from the other end of
the schooner.

A DISCIPLINARIAN

"THERE'S no doubt about it," said the night watchman, "but what dissipline's a very good thing, but it don't always act well. For instance, I ain't allowed to smoke on this wharf, so when I want a pipe I either 'ave to go over to the 'Queen's 'ed,' or sit in a lighter. If I'm in the 'Queen's 'ed' I can't look arter the wharf, an' once when I was sitting in a lighter smoking the chap come aboard an' cast off afore I knew what he was doing, an' took me all the way to Greenwich. He said he'd often played that trick on watchmen.

"The worst man for dissipline I ever shipped with was Cap'n Tasker, of the *Lapwing*. He'd got it on the brain bad. He was a prim, clean-shaved man except for a little side-whisker, an' always used to try an' look as much like a naval officer as possible.

"I never 'ad no sort of idea what he was like when I jined the ship, an' he was quite quiet and peaceable until we was out in the open water.

Then the cloven hoof showed itself, an' he kicked one o' the men for coming on deck with a dirty face, an' though the man told him he never did wash becos his skin was so delikit, he sent the bos'en to turn the hose on him.

"The bos'en seemed to take a hand in everything. We used to do everything by his whistle, it was never out of his mouth scarcely, and I've known that man to dream of it o' nights, and sit up in his sleep an' try an' blow his thumb. He whistled us to swab decks, whistled us to grub, whistled us to every blessed thing.

"Though we didn't belong to any reg'ler line, we'd got a lot o' passengers aboard, going to the Cape, an' they thought a deal o' the skipper. There was one young leftenant aboard who said he reminded him o' Nelson, an' him an' the skipper was as thick as two thieves. Nice larky young chap he was, an' more than one o' the crew tried to drop things on him from aloft when he wasn't looking.

"Every morning at ten we was inspected by the skipper, but that wasn't enough for the leftenant, and he persuaded the old man to drill us. He said it would do us good an' amuse the passengers, an' we 'ad to do all sorts o' silly things with our arms an' legs, an' twice he walked the skipper to the other end of the ship, leaving twenty-three sailormen bending over touching their toes, an' wondering whether they 'd ever stand straight again.

"The very worst thing o' the lot was the boat-drill. A chap might be sitting comfortable at his grub, or having a pipe in his bunk, when the bos'en's whistle would scream out to him that the ship was sinking, an' the passengers drownding, and he was to come an' git the boats out an' save 'em. Nice sort o' game it was too. We had to run like mad with kegs o' water an' bags o' biscuit, an' then run the boats out an' launch 'em. All the men were told off to certain boats, an' the passengers too. The only difference was, if a passenger didn't care about taking a hand in the game he didn't, but we had to.

"One o' the passengers who didn't play was Major Miggens. He was very much agin it, an' called it tomfoolery; he never would go to his boat, but used to sit and sneer all the time.

"'It's only teaching the men to cut an' run,' he, said to the skipper one day; "'if there ever was any need they'd run to the boats an' leave us here. Don't tell me.'

"'That's not the way I should ha' expected to hear you speak of British sailors, major,' ses the skipper rather huffy.

"'British *swearers*,' ses the major, sniffing. 'You don't hear their remarks when that whistle is blown.   It's enough to bring a judgment on the ship.'

"'If you can point 'em out to me I'll punish 'em,' says the skipper very warm.

"'I'm not going to point 'em out,' ses the major. 'I symperthise with 'em too much.   They don't get any of their beauty sleep, pore chaps, an' they want it, every one of 'em.'

"I thought that was a very kind remark o' the major to make, but o' course some of the wimmin larfed.   I s'pose they think men don't want beauty sleep, as it's called.

"I heard the leftenant symperthising with the skipper arter that.   He said the major was simply jealous because the men drilled so beautifully, an' then they walked aft, the leftenant talking very earnest an' the skipper shaking his head at something he was saying.

"It was just two nights arter this.   I'd gone below an' turned in when I began to dream that the major had borrowed the bos'en's whistle an' was practising on it.   I remember thinking in my sleep what a comfort it was it was only the major, when one of the chaps give me a dig in the back an' woke me.

"'Tumble up,' ses he, 'the ship's afire.'

"I rushed up on deck, an' there was no mistake about who was blowing the whistle   The bell was jangling horrible, smoke was rolling up from the hatches, an' some o' the men was dragging out the hose an' tripping up the passengers with it as they came running up on deck. The noise and confusion was fearful.

"'Out with the boats,' ses Tom Hall to me, 'don't you hear the whistle?'

"'What, ain't we going to try an' put the fire out?' I ses.

"'Obey orders,' ses Tom, 'that's what we've got to do, an' the sooner we're away the better. You know what's in her.'

"We ran to the boats then, an', I must say, we got 'em out well, and the very fust person to git into mine was the major in his piejammers; arter all the others was in we 'ad 'im out agin. He didn't belong to our boat, an' dissipline is dissipline any day.

"Afore we could git clear o' the ship, however, he came yelling to the side an' said *his* boat had gone, an' though we prodded him with our oars he lowered himself over the side and dropped in.

"Fortunately for us it was a lovely clear night; there was no moon, but the stars were very bright. The engines had stopped, an' the old ship sat on the water scarcely moving. Another boat was bumping up against ours, and two more came creeping round the bows from the port side an' jined us.

"'Who's in command?' calls out the major.

"'I am,' ses the first mate very sharp-like from one of the boats.

"'Where's the cap'n then?' called out an old lady from my boat o' the name o' Prendergast.

"'He's standing by the ship,' ses the mate.

"'Doing *what?*' ses Mrs. Prendergast, looking at the water as though she expected to see the skipper standing there.

"'He's going down with the ship,' ses one o' the chaps.

"Then Mrs. Prendergast asked somebody to be kind enough to lend her a handkerchief, becos she had left her pocket behind aboard ship, and began to sob very bitter.

"'Just a simple British sailor,' ses she, snivelling, 'going down with his ship. There he is. Look! On the bridge.'

"We all looked, an' then some o' the other wimmin wanted to borrer handkerchiefs. I lent one of 'em a little cotton waste, but she was so unpleasant about its being a trifle oily that she forgot all about crying, and said she'd tell the mate about me as soon as ever we got ashore.

"'I'll remember him in my prayers,' ses one o'

the wimmin who was crying comfortable in a big red bandana belonging to one o' the men.

"'All England shall ring with his deed,' ses another.

"'Sympathy's cheap,' ses one of the men passengers solemnly. 'If we ever reach land we must all band together to keep his widow an' orphans.'

"'Hear, hear,' cries everybody.

"'And we'll put up a granite tombstone to his memory,' ses Mrs. Prendergast.

"'S'pose we pull back to the ship an' take him off,' ses a gentleman from another boat. 'I'm thinking it 'ud come cheaper, an' perhaps the puir mon would really like it better himself.'

"'Shame,' ses most of 'em; an' I reely b'leeve they'd worked theirselves up to that pitch they'd ha' felt disapponted if the skipper had been saved.

"We pulled along slowly, the mate's boat leading, looking back every now and then at the old ship, and wondering when she would go off, for she'd got that sort o' stuff in her hold which 'ud send her up with a bang as soon as the fire got to it; an' we was all waiting for the shock.

"'Do you know where we're going, Mr. Bunce?' calls out the major.

"'Yes,' ses the mate.

"'What's the nearest land?' asks the major.

"''Bout a thousand miles,' ses the mate.

"Then the major went into figgers, an' worked out that it 'ud take us about ten days to reach land and three to reach the bottom o' the water kegs. He shouted that out to the mate; an' the young leftenant what was in the mate's boat smoking a big cigar said there'd be quite a run on granite tombstones. He said it was a blessed thing he had disinherited his children for marrying agin his wishes, so there wouldn't be any orphans left to mourn for him.

"Some o' the wimmin smiled a little at this, an' old Mrs. Prendergast shook so that she made the boat rock. We got quite cheerful somehow, and one of the other men spoke up and said that owing to his only having reckoned two pints to the gallon, the major's figgers wasn't to be relied upon.

"We got more cheerful then, and we was beginning to look on it as just a picnic, when I'm blest if the mate's boat didn't put about and head for the ship agin.

"There was a commotion then if you like, everybody talking and laughing at once; and Mrs. Prendergast said that such a thing as one single-handed cap'n staying behind to go down with his ship, and then putting the fire out all by himself

after his men had fled, had never been heard
of before, an' she believed it never would be again.
She said he must be terribly burnt, and he'd
have to be put to bed and wrapped up in oily
rags.

"It didn't take us long to get aboard agin, and
the ladies fairly mobbed the skipper. Tom Hall
swore as 'ow Mrs. Prendergast tried to kiss him, an'
the fuss they made of him was ridiculous. I heard
the clang of the telegraph in the engine-room soon
as the boats was hoisted up, the engines started,
and off we went again.

"'Speech,' yells out somebody. 'Speech.'

"'Bravo!' ses the others. 'Bravo!'

"Then the skipper stood up an' made 'em a nice
little speech. First of all he thanked 'em for their
partiality and kindness shown to him, and the
orderly way in which they had left the ship. He
said it reflected credit on all concerned, crew and
passengers, an' no doubt they'd be surprised when
he told them that there hadn't been any fire at all,
but that it was just a test to make sure that the
boat drill was properly understood.

"He was quite right about them being surprised.
Noisy, too, they was, an' the things they said about
the man they'd just been wanting to give granite
tombstones to was simply astonishing. It would
have taken a whole cemetery o' tombstones to put

down all they said about him, and then they'd ha' had to cut the letters small.

"'I vote we have an indignation meeting in the saloon to record our disgust at the cap'n's behaviour,' ses the major fiercely. 'I beg to propose that Mr. Macpherson take the chair.'

"'I second that,' ses another, fierce-like.

"'I beg to propose the major instead,' ses somebody else in a heasy off-hand sort o' way; 'Mr. Macpherson's boat not having come back yet.'

"At first everybody thought he was joking, but when they found he was really speaking the truth the excitement was awful. Fortunately, as Mrs. Prendergast remarked, there was no ladies in the boat, but there was several men passengers. We were doing a good thirteen knots an hour, but we brought up at once, an' then we 'ad the most lovely firework display I ever see aboard ship in my life. Blue lights and rockets and guns going all night, while we cruised slowly about, and the passengers sat on deck arguing as to whether the skipper would be hung or only imprisoned for life.

"It was daybreak afore we sighted them, just a little speck near the sky-line, an' we bore down on them for all we was worth. Half an hour later they was alongside, an' of all the chilly, miserable-looking men I ever see they was the worst.

"They had to be helped up the side a'most, and

they was so grateful it was quite affecting, until the true state o' things was explained to them. It seemed to change 'em wonderful, an' after Mr. Macpherson had had three cups o' hot coffee an' four glasses o' brandy he took the chair at the indignation meeting, an' went straight off to sleep in it. They woke him up three times, but he was so cross about it that the ladies had to go away an' the meeting was adjourned.

"I don't think it ever came to much after all, nobody being really hurt, an' the skipper being so much upset they felt sort o' sorry for 'im.

"The rest of the passage was very quiet an' comfortable, but o' course it all came out at the other end, an' the mate brought the ship home. Some o' the chaps said the skipper was a bit wrong in the 'ed, and, while I'm not gainsaying that, it's my firm opinion that he was persuaded to do what he did by that young leftenant. As I said afore, he was a larky young chap, an' very fond of a joke if he didn't have to pay for it."

BROTHER HUTCHINS

" I 'VE got a friend coming down with us this trip, George," said the master of the *Wave*, as they sat on deck after tea watching the river. "One of our new members, Brother Hutchins."

"From the Mission, I s'pose?" said the mate coldly.

"From the Mission," confirmed the skipper. "You'll like him, George; he's been one o' the greatest rascals that ever breathed."

"Well, I don't know what you mean," said the mate, looking up indignantly.

"He's 'ad a most interestin' life," said the skipper; "he's been in half the jails of England. To hear 'im talk is as good as reading a book. And 'e's as merry as they make 'em."

"Oh, and is 'e goin' to give us prayers afore breakfast like that fat-necked, white-faced old rascal what came down with us last summer and stole my boots?" demanded the mate.

"He never stole 'em, George," said the skipper.
"If you'd 'eard that man cry when I mentioned
to 'im your unjust suspicions, you'd never have
forgiven yourself. He told 'em at the meetin', an'
they had prayers for you."

"You an' your Mission are a pack o' fools,"
said the mate scornfully. "You're always being
done. A man comes to you an' ses 'e's found
grace, and you find 'im a nice, easy, comfortable
living. 'E sports a bit of blue ribbon and a red
nose at the same time. Don't tell me. You
ask me why I don't join you, and I tell you
it's because I don't want to lose my common
sense."

"You'll know better one o' these days, George,"
said the skipper, rising. "I earnestly hope you'll
'ave some great sorrow or affliction, something
almost too great for you to bear. It's the only
thing that'll save you."

"I expect that fat chap what stole my boots
would like to see it too," said the mate.

"He would," said the skipper solemnly. "He
said so."

The mate got up, fuming and knocking his pipe
out with great violence against the side of the
schooner, stamped up and down the deck two
or three times, and then, despairing of regaining
his accustomed calm on board, went ashore.

It was late when he returned. A light burnt in the cabin, and the skipper with his spectacles on was reading aloud from an old number of the *Evangelical Magazine* to a thin, white-faced man dressed in black.

"That's my mate," said the skipper, looking up from his book.

"Is he one of our band?" inquired the stranger.

The skipper shook his head despondently.

"Not yet," said the stranger encouragingly.

"Seen too many of 'em," said the mate bluntly. " The more I see of 'em, the less I like 'em. It makes me feel wicked to look at 'em."

"Ah, that ain't you speaking now, it's the Evil One," said Mr. Hutchins confidently.

"I s'pose you know 'im pretty well," said the mate simply.

"I lived with him thirty years," said Mr. Hutchins solemnly, "then I got tired of him."

"I should think he got a bit sick too," said the mate. "Thirty days 'ud ha' been too long for me."

He went to his berth, to give Mr. Hutchins time to frame a suitable reply, and returned with a full bottle of whisky and a tumbler, and having drawn the cork with a refreshing pop, mixed himself a stiff glass and lit his pipe. Mr. Hutchins with a deep groan gazed reproachfully at the skipper and shook his head at the bottle.

"You know I don't like you to bring that filthy stuff in the cabin, George," said the skipper.

"It's not for me," said the mate flippantly. "It's for the Evil One. He ses the sight of his old pal 'Utchins 'as turned his stomach."

He glanced at the stranger and saw to his astonishment that he appeared to be struggling with a strong desire to laugh. His lips tightened and his shifty little eyes watered, but he conquered himself in a moment, and rising to his feet delivered a striking address in favour of teetotalism. He condemned whisky as not only wicked, but unnecessary, declaring with a side glance at the mate that two acidulated drops dissolved in water were an excellent substitute.

The sight of the whisky appeared to madden him, and the skipper sat spell-bound at his eloquence, until at length, after apostrophizing the bottle in a sentence which left him breathless, he snatched it up and dashed it to pieces on the floor.

For a moment the mate was struck dumb with fury, then with a roar he leaped up and rushed for the lecturer, but the table was between them, and before he could get over it the skipper sprang up and seizing him by the arm, pushed his friend into the state-room.

"Lea' go," foamed the mate. "Let me get at him."

"George," said the skipper, still striving with him, "I'm ashamed of you."

"Ashamed be damned," yelled the mate, struggling. "What did he chuck my whisky away for?"

"He's a saint," said the skipper, relaxing his hold as he heard Mr. Hutchins lock himself in. "He's a saint, George. Seein' 'is beautiful words 'ad no effect on you, he 'ad recourse to strong measures."

"Wait till I get hold of 'im," said the mate menacingly. "Only wait, I'll saint 'im."

"Is he better, dear friend?" came the voice of Mr. Hutchins from beyond the door; "because I forgot the tumbler."

"Come out," roared the mate, "come out and upset it."

Mr. Hutchins declined the invitation, but from behind the door pleaded tearfully with the mate to lead a better life, and even rebuked the skipper for allowing the bottle of sin to be produced in the cabin. The skipper took the rebuke humbly, and after requesting Mr. Hutchins to sleep in the state-room that night in order to frustrate the evident designs of the mate, went on deck for a final look round and then came below and turned in himself.

The crew of the schooner were early astir next morning getting under way, but Mr. Hutchins kept his bed, although the mate slipped down to the cabin several times and tapped at his door. When he did come up the mate was at the wheel and the men down below getting breakfast.

"Sleep well?" inquired Mr. Hutchins softly, as he took a seat on the hatches, a little distance from him.

"I'll let you know when I haven't got this wheel," said the mate sourly.

"Do," said Mr. Hutchins genially. "We shall see you at our meeting to-night?" he asked blandly.

The mate disdained to reply, but his wrath when at Mr. Hutchins' request the cabin was invaded by the crew that evening, cannot be put into words.

For three nights they had what Mr. Hutchins described as love-feasts, and the mate as blamed bear-gardens. The crew were not particularly partial to hymns, considered as such, but hymns shouted out with the full force of their lungs while sharing the skipper's hymn-book appealed

to them strongly.   Besides, it maddened the
mate, and to know that they were defying their
superior, and at the same time doing good to
their own souls, was very sweet.   The boy,
whose voice was just breaking, got off some
surprising effects, and seemed to compass about
five octaves without distress.

When they were exhausted with singing Mr.
Hutchins would give them a short address,
generally choosing as his subject a strong, violent-
tempered man given to drink and coarse language.
The speaker proved conclusively that a man who
drank would do other things in secret, and he
pictured this man going home and beating his
wife because she reproached him for breaking
open the children's money - box to spend the
savings on Irish whisky.   At every point he
made he groaned, and the crew, as soon as they
found they might groan too, did so with extraordinary gusto, the boy's groans being weird
beyond conception.

They reached Plymouth, where they had to
put out a few cases of goods, just in time to
save the mate's reason, for the whole ship,
owing to Mr. Hutchins' zeal, was topsy turvy.
The ship's cat sat up all one night cursing him
and a blue ribbon he had tied round her neck,
and even the battered old tea-pot came down

to meals bedizened with bows of the same proselytizing hue.

By the time they had got to their moorings it was too late to take the hatches off, and the crew sat gazing longingly at the lights ashore. Their delight when the visitor obtained permission for them to go ashore with him for a little stroll was unbounded, and they set off like schoolboys.

"They couldn't be with a better man," said the skipper, as the party moved off; "when I think of the good that man's done in under four days it makes me ashamed of myself."

"You'd better ship 'im as mate," said George. "There'd be a pair of you then."

"There's greater work for 'im to do," said the skipper solemnly.

He saw the mate's face in the waning light, and moved off with a sigh. The mate, for his part, leaned against the side smoking, and as the skipper declined to talk on any subject but Mr. Hutchins, relapsed into a moody silence until the return of the crew some two hours later.

"Mr. Hutchins is coming on after, sir," said the boy. "He told us to say he was paying a visit to a friend."

"What's the name of the pub?" asked the mate quietly.

"If you can't speak without showing your nasty temper, George, you'd better hold your tongue," said the skipper severely. "What's your opinion about Mr. Hutchins, my lads?"

"A more open 'arted man never breathed," said Dan, the oldest of the crew, warmly.

"Best feller I ever met in my life," said another.

"You hear that?" said the skipper.

"I hear," said the mate.

"'E's a Christian," said the boy. "I never knew what a Christian was before I met 'im. What do you think 'e give us?"

"Give you?" said the skipper.

"A pound cash," said the boy. "A golden sovring each. Tork about Christians! I wish I knew a few more of 'em."

"Well I never!" exclaimed the gratified skipper.

"An' the way 'e did it was so nice," said the oldest seaman. "'E ses, 'That's from me an' the skipper,' 'e ses. 'Thank the skipper for it as much as me,' 'e ses."

"Well now, don't waste it," said the skipper. "I should bank it if I was you. It'll make a nice little nest-egg."

"I 'ope it was come by honest, that's all," said the mate.

"O' course it was," cried the skipper. "You've

got a 'ard, cruel 'art, George. P'raps if it 'ad been
a little softer you'd 'ave 'ad one too."

"Blast 'is sovrings," said the surly mate. "I'd
like to know where he got 'em from, an' wot
'e means by saying it come from you as much
as 'im. I never knew *you* to give money
away."

"I s'pose," said the skipper very softly, "he
means that I put such-like thoughts into 'is 'art.
Well, you'd better turn in, my lads. We start
work at four."

The hands went forward, and the skipper and
mate descended to the cabin and prepared for
sleep. The skipper set a lamp on the table ready
for Mr. Hutchins when he should return, and after
a short inward struggle bade the mate "good-
night," and in a couple of minutes was fast
asleep.

At four o'clock the mate woke suddenly to find
the skipper standing by his berth. The lamp
still stood burning on the table, fighting feebly
against the daylight which was pouring in through
the skylight.

"Not turned up yet?" said the mate, with a
glance at the visitor's empty berth.

The skipper shook his head spiritlessly and
pointed to the table. The mate following his
finger, saw a small canvas bag, and by the side

of it fourpence halfpenny in coppers and an unknown amount in brace buttons.

"There was twenty-three pounds freight money in that bag when we left London," said the skipper, finding his voice at last.

"Well, what do you think's become of it?" inquired the mate, taking up the lamp and blowing it out.

"I can't think," said the skipper, "my 'ed's all confused. Bro—Mr. Hutchins ain't come back yet."

"I s'pose he was late and didn't like to disturb you," said the mate without moving a muscle, "but I've no doubt 'e's all right. Don't you worry about him."

"It's very strange where it's gone, George," faltered the skipper, "very strange."

"Well, 'Utchins is a generous sort o' chap," said the mate, "'e give the men five pounds for nothing, so perhaps he'll give you something—when 'e comes back."

"Go an' ask the crew to come down here," said the skipper, sinking on a locker and gazing at the brazen collection before him.

The mate obeyed, and a few minutes afterwards returned with the men, who, swarming into the cabin, listened sympathetically as the skipper related his loss.

"It's a mystery which nobody can understand, sir," said old Dan when he had finished, "and it's no use tryin'."

"One o' them things what won't never be cleared up properly," said the cook comfortably.

"Well, I don't like to say it," said the skipper, "but I must. The only man who could have taken it was Hutchins."

"Wot, sir," said Dan, "that blessed man! Why, I'd laugh at the idea."

"He couldn't do it," said the boy, "not if he tried he couldn't. He was too good."

"He's taken that twenty-three poun'," said the skipper deliberately; "eighteen, we'll call it, because I'm goin' to have five of it back."

"You're labourin' under a great mistake, sir," said Dan ambiguously.

"Are you going to give me that money?" said the skipper loudly.

"Beggin' your pardon, sir, no," said the cook, speaking for the rest, as he put his foot on the companion-ladder. "Brother 'Utchins gave us that money for singing them 'ims so well. 'E said so, and we ain't 'ad no call to think as it warn't honestly come by. Nothing could ever make us think that, would it, mates?"

"Nothing," said the others with exemplary firmness. "It couldn't be done."

They followed the cook up on deck, and leaning over the side, gazed in a yearning fashion toward the place where they had last seen their bene-factor.   Then with a sorrowful presentiment that they would never look upon his like again, they turned away and prepared for the labours of the day.

THE DISBURSEMENT SHEET

THE old man was dead, and his son Edward reigned in his stead. The old man had risen from a humble position in life; his rule was easy, and his manner of conducting business eminently approved of by the rough old seamen who sailed his small craft round the coast, and by that sharp clerk Simmons, on whose discovery the old man was wont, at times, to hug himself in secret. The proceedings, when one of his skippers came home from a voyage, were severely simple. The skipper would produce a bag, and, emptying it upon the table, give an account of his voyage; whenever he came to an expenditure, raking the sum out of the heap, until, at length, the cash was divided into two portions, one of which went to the owner, the other to the skipper.

But other men other manners. The books of the inimitable Simmons being overhauled, revealed the startling fact that they were kept by single entry; in addition to which, a series of dots and dashes appeared against the figures forming a code, the only key to which was locked up somewhere in Simmons's interior.

"It's a wonder the firm hasn't gone bankrupt long ago," said the new governor, after the clerk had explained the meaning of various signs and wonders. "What does this starfish against the entry mean?"

"It isn't a starfish, sir," said Simmons; "it means that one bag of sugar got wetted a little; then, if the consignees notice it, we shall know we have got to allow for it."

"A pretty way of doing business, upon my word. It'll all have to be altered," said the other. "I must have new offices too; this dingy little hole is enough to frighten people away."

The conversation was interrupted by the entrance of Captain Fazackerly, of the schooner *Sarah Ann*, who, having just brought up in the river, had hastened to the office to report.

"Mornin', sir," said the captain respectfully; "I'm glad to see you here, sir, but the office don't seem real like without your father sitting in it. He was a good master, and we're all sorry to lose him."

"You're very good," said the new master somewhat awkwardly.

"I expect it'll take some time for you to get into the way of it," said the captain, with a view to giving the conversation a more cheerful turn.

"I expect it will," said the new master, thinking of the starfish.

"It's a mercy Simmons wasn't took too," said the captain, shaking his head. "As it is, he's spared; he'll be able to teach you. There ain't" —he lowered his voice, not wishing to make Simmons unduly proud—"there ain't a smarter clerk in all Liverpool than wot he is."

"I'm glad to hear it," said the new master, regarding the old man with raised eyebrows, as he extricated a plethoric-looking canvas bag from his jacket pocket and dropped it with a musical crash on the chipped office table. His eyebrows went still higher, as the old man unfastened the string, and emptying the contents on to the table, knitted his brows into reflective wrinkles, and began to debit the firm with all the liabilities of a slow but tenacious memory.

"Oh, come," said the owner sharply, as the old man lovingly hooked out the sum of five-and-sixpence as a first instalment, "this won't do, cap'n."

"Wot won't do, Mas'r Edward?" inquired the old man in surprise.

"Why this way of doing business," said the other. "It's not businesslike at all, you know."

"Well, it's the way me an' your pore old father has done it this last thirty year," said the skipper, "an' I'm sure I've never knowingly cheated him out of a ha'penny; and a better man o' business than your father never breathed."

"Yes; well, I'm going to do things a bit differently," said the new master. "You must give me a proper disbursement sheet, cap'n, if you please."

"And what may that be?" inquired Captain Fazackerly, as with great slowness he gathered up the money and replaced it in the bag; "I never heard of it afore."

"Well, I haven't got time to teach you book-keeping," said the other, somewhat nettled at the old man's manner. "Can't you get some of your brother captains to show you? Some deep-sea man would be sure to know."

"I'll see what I can do, sir," said the skipper slowly, as he turned towards the door. "My word was always good enough for your father."

In a moody, indignant frame of mind he stuck his hands furiously in his trousers' pockets, and passed heavily through the swing-doors. At other times he had been wont to take a genial, if heavy interest in passing events; but, in this instance, he plodded on, dwelling darkly upon his grievance, until he reached, by the mere force of habit, a certain favourite tavern. He pulled up sharply, and, as a mere matter of duty and custom, and not because he wanted it, went in and ordered a glass of gin.

He drank three, and was so hazy in his replies to the young lady behind the bar, usually a prime favourite, that she took offence, and availing herself, for private reasons, of a public weapon, coldly declined to serve him with a fourth.

"Wot?" said the astounded Fazackerly, coming out of his haze.

"You've had enough!" said the girl firmly. "You get aboard again, *and mind how you do so.*"

The skipper gazed at her for a moment in open-mouthed horror, and then jamming his hat firmly over his brows, stumbled out of the door and into the street, where he ran full into the arms of another mariner who was just entering.

"Why, Zacky, my boy," cried the latter, clapping him lustily on the back, "how goes it?"

In broken, indignant accents the other told him.

"You come in with me," said the new-comer.

"I'll never enter that pub again," said the skipper.

"You come in with me," said the master-mind firmly.

Captain Fazackerly hesitated a moment, and then, feeling that he was safe in the hands of the master of a foreign-going barque, followed him into the bar, and from behind his back glared defiantly at his fair foe.

"Two glasses o' gin, my dear," said Captain Tweedie with the slightest possible emphasis.

The girl, who knew her customer, served him without a murmur, deftly avoiding the gaze of ungenerous triumph with which the injured captain favoured her as he raised the cooling beverage to his lips. The glass emptied, he placed it on the counter and sighed despondently.

"There's something up with you, Zacky," said Tweedie, eyeing him closely as he bit the end off a cigar; "you've got something on your mind."

"I've been crool hurt," said his friend in a hard, cold voice. "My word ain't good enough for the new guv'nor; he wants what he calls a disbursement sheet."

"Well, give him one," said Tweedie. "You know what it is, don't you?"

Captain Fazackerly shook his head, and pushing the glasses along the counter nodded for them to be refilled.

"You come aboard with me," said Tweedie after they had emptied them.

Captain Fazackerly, who had a doglike faith in his friend, followed him into the street and on to his barque. In a general way he experienced a social rise when he entered the commodious cabin of that noble craft, and his face grew in importance as his host, after motioning him to a seat, placed a select array of writing materials before him.

"I s'pose I've got to do it," he said slowly.

"Of course you have," said Tweedie, rolling his cigar between his thin lips; "you've got orders to do so, haven't you? We must all obey those above us. What would you do if one of your men refused to obey an order of yours?"

"Hit him in the face," said Captain Fazackerly with simple directness.

"Just so," said Tweedie, who was always ready to impart moral teaching. "And when your governor asks for a disbursement sheet you've got to give him one. Now, then, head that paper—Voyage of the *Sarah Ann*, 180 tons register, Garston Docks to Limerick."

The captain squared his elbows, and, for a few seconds, nothing was heard but his stertorous breathing and the scratching of the pen; then a muttered execration, and Captain Fazackerly put down his pen with a woe-begone air.

"What's the matter?" said Tweedie.

"I've spelt register without the 'd,'" said the other; "that's what comes o' being worried."

"It don't matter," said Tweedie hastily. "Now what about stores? Wait a bit, though; of course ye repaired your side-lamps before starting?"

"Lor', no!" said Captain Fazackerly, staring; "what for? They were all right."

"Ye lie," said Tweedie sternly, "you did! To repairs to side-lamps, ten shillings. Now then, did you paint her this trip?"

"I did," said the other, looking at the last entry in a fascinated fashion.

"Let's see," said Tweedie meditatively—"we'll say five gallons of black varnish at one shilling and threepence a gallon——"

"No, no," said the scribe; "I used gas tar at threepence a gallon."

"Five gallons black varnish, one shilling and threepence a gallon, six-and-threepence," said Tweedie, raising his voice a little; "have you got that down?"

After a prolonged struggle with his feelings the other said he had.

"Twenty-eight pounds black paint at twopence a pound," continued Tweedie.

"Nay, nay," said the skipper; "I allus saves the soot out of the galley for that."

The other captain took his cigar from his lips and gazed severely at his guest.

"Am I dealing with a chimney-sweep or a ship's captain?" he inquired plaintively; "it would simplify matters a bit if I knew."

"Go on, Captain Tweedie," said the other, turning a fine purple colour; "how much did you say it was?"

"Twenty-eight twos equals fifty-six; that's four-and-ninepence," continued Tweedie, his face relaxing to receive the cigar again; "and twenty-eight pounds white lead at twenty-eight shillings a hundredweight——"

"Three penn'orth o' whiting's good enough for me, matey," said Captain Fazackerly, making a stand.

"See here," said Tweedie, "who's making out this disbursement sheet, you or me?"

"You are," said the other.

"Very good then," said his friend; "now don't you interrupt. I don't mind telling you, you must never use rubbish o' that sort in a disbursement sheet. It looks bad for the firm. If any other owners saw that in your old man's sheet he'd never hear the end of it, and he'd never forgive you. That'll be—what did I say? Seven shillings. And now we come to the voyage. Ye had a tug to give ye a pluck out to the bar?"

"No; we went out with a fair wind," said Captain Fazackerly, toying with his pen.

"Ye lie; ye had a tug out to the bar," repeated Tweedie wearily.   "Did ye share the towing?"

"Why, no, I tell 'e——"

"That'll be three pounds then," said Tweedie. "If ye'd shared it it would have been two pound ten.   You should always study your owner in these matters, cap'n.   Now, what about bad weather?   Any repairs to the sails?"

"Ay, we had a lot o' damage," said Fazackerly, laying down his pen; "it took us days to repair 'em.   Cost us four pounds.   We had to put into Holyhead for shelter."

"Four pounds!" said Tweedie, his voice rising almost to a scream.

"Ay, all that," said Fazackerly very solemnly.

"Look here," said Tweedie in a choked voice. "Blown away fore lower topsail, fore-staysail, and carried away lifts to staysail.   To sailmaker for above, eleven pounds eighteen shillings and ten-pence.   Then ye say ye put into Holyhead for shelter.   Well, here in entering harbour we'll say loss of port anchor and thirty fathoms of chain cable——"

"Man alive," said the overwrought skipper, hitting the table heavily with his fist, "the old anchor's there for him to see."

"To divers for recovering same, and placing on deck, two pound ten," continued Tweedie, raising his voice. "Did you do any damage going into dock at Limerick?"

"More than we've done for years," said Fazackerly, and shaking his head, entered into voluminous details; "total, seven pounds."

"Seven pounds!" said the exasperated Tweedie. "Seven pounds for all that, and your insurance don't begin till twenty-five pounds. Why, damme, you ain't fit to be trusted out with a ship. I firmly b'lieve if you lost her you'd send in a bill for a suit of clothes, and call it square. Now take this down, and larn a business way o' doing things. In entering dock, carried away starboard cathead and started starboard chain plates; held survey of damage done: decided to take off channel bends, renew through bolts, straighten plates and replace same; also to renew cathead and caulk ship's side in wake of plate, six seams, &c. &c. There, now, that looks better. Twenty-seven pounds eighteen and sevenpence halfpenny, and I think, for all that damage, it's a very reasonable bill. Can you remember anything else?"

"You've got a better memory than I have," said his admiring friend. "Wait a bit, though; yes, I had my poor old dog washed overboard."

"Dog!" said the deep-sea man; "we can't put dogs in a disbursement sheet. 'Tain't business."

"My old master would have given me another one, though," grumbled Fazackerly. "I wouldn't ha' parted with that dog for anything. He knew as much as you or me, that dog did. I never knew him to bite an officer, but I don't think there was ever a man came on the ship but what he'd have a bit out of, sooner or later."

"Them sort of dogs do get washed overboard," said Tweedie impatiently.

"Boys he couldn't abear," pursued the other, in tones of tender reminiscence; "the mere sight of a boarding-school of 'em out for a walk would give him hydrophoby almost."

"Just so," said Tweedie. "Ah! there's cork fenders; ye may pick them up floating down the river, or they may come aboard in the night from a craft alongside; they're changeable sort o' things, but in the disbursement sheet they must go, and best quality too, four-and-sixpence each. Anything else?"

"There's the dog," said Fazackerly persistently.

"Copper nails, tenpence," said Tweedie the dictator.

"Haven't bought any for months," said the other, but slowly entering it.

"Well, it ain't exactly right," said Tweedie, shrugging his shoulders, "but you're so set on him going in."

"Him? Who?" asked Captain Fazackerly, staring.

"The dog," said Tweedie; "if he goes in as copper nails, he won't be noticed."

"If he goes in as tenpence, I'm a Dutchman," said the bereaved owner, scoring out the copper nails. "You never knew that dog properly, Tweedie."

"Well, never mind about the dog," said Tweedie; "let's cast the sheet. What do you think it comes to?"

"'Bout thirty pun'," hazarded the other.

"Thirty fiddlesticks," retorted Tweedie; "there you are in black and white—sixty-three pounds eighteen shillings and tenpence ha'penny."

"And is that what Mas'r Edward wants?" inquired Captain Fazackerly, gasping.

"Yes; that's a properly drawn up disbursement sheet," said Tweedie in satisfied tones. "You see how it simplifies matters. The governor can see at a glance how things stand, while, if you trusted to your memory, you might forget something, or else claim something you didn't have."

"I ought to have had them things afore," said

Captain Fazackerly, shaking his head solemnly. "I'd ha' been riding in my carriage by now."

"Never ye dream of having another v'y'ge without one," said Tweedie. "I doubt whether it's lawful to render an account without one."

He folded the paper, and handed it to his friend, who, after inspecting it with considerable pride, tucked it carefully away in his breast pocket.

"Take it up in the morning," said Tweedie. "We'll have a bit o' tea down here, and then we'll go round a bit afterwards."

Captain Fazackerly having no objection, they had tea first, and then, accompanied by the first mate, went out to christen the disbursement sheet. The ceremony, which was of great length, was solemnly impressive towards the finish. Captain Tweedie, who possessed a very sensitive, highly-strung nature, finding it necessary to put a licensed victualler out of his own house before it could be completed to his satisfaction.

The one thing which Captain Fazackerly remembered clearly the next morning when he awoke was the disbursement sheet. He propped it against the coffee-pot during breakfast, and read selections to his admiring mate, and after a refreshing toilet, proceeded to the office. Simmons was already there, and before the skipper could get to the purpose of his visit, the head of the firm arrived.

"I've just brought the disbursement sheet you asked for, sir," said the skipper, drawing it from his pocket.

"Ah! you've got it, then," said the new governor, with a gracious smile; "you see it wasn't so much trouble after all."

"I don't mind the trouble, sir," interrupted Captain Fazackerly.

"You see it puts things on a better footing," said the other. "I can see at a glance now how things stand, and Simmons can enter the items straight away into the books of the firm. It's more satisfactory to both of us. Sit down, cap'n."

The captain sat down, his face glowing with this satisfactory recognition of his work.

"I met Cap'n Hargreaves as I was a-coming up," he said; "and I explained to him your ideas on the subject, an' he went straight back, as straight as he could go, to make out *his* disbursement sheet."

"Ah! we shall soon have things on a better footing now," said the governor, unfolding the paper, while the skipper gazed abstractedly through the small, dirty panes of the office window at the bustle on the quay below.

For a short space there was silence in the office, broken only by the half-audible interjections of the reader. Then he spoke.

"Simmons!" he said sharply.

The old clerk slipped from his stool, and obeying the motions of his employer inspected, in great astonishment, the first disbursement sheet which had ever entered the office. He read through every item in an astonished whisper, and, having finished, followed the governor's example and gazed at the heavy figure by the window.

"Captain Fazackerly," said his employer, at length, breaking a painful silence.

"Sir," said the captain, turning his head a little.

"I've been talking with Simmons about these disbursement sheets," said the owner, somewhat awkwardly; "Simmons is afraid they'll give him a lot of extra trouble."

The captain turned his head a little more, and gazed stolidly at the astonished Simmons.

"A man oughtn't to mind a little extra trouble if the firm wishes it," he said somewhat severely.

"He's afraid it would throw his books out a bit," continued the owner, deftly avoiding the gaze of the injured clerk. "You see, Simmons' book-keeping is of the old-fashioned kind, cap'n, star-fishes and all that kind of thing," he continued, incoherently, as the gaze of Simmons, refusing to be longer avoided, broke the thread of his discourse. "So I think we'll put the paper on the fire, cap'n, and do business in the old way. Have you got the money with you?"

"I have, sir," said Fazackerly, feeling in his pocket, as he mournfully watched his last night's work blazing up the chimney.

"Fire away, then," said the owner, almost cordially.

Captain Fazackerly advanced to the table, and clearing his throat, fixed his eyes in a reflective stare on the opposite wall and commenced:—

"Blown away fore lower topsail, fore-staysail, and carried away lifts to staysail. To sailmaker for above, eleven pounds eighteen shillings and tenpence," he said, with relish. "Tug out to the bar, three pounds. To twenty-eight pounds black soot, I mean paint——"

RULE OF THREE

THE long summer day had gone and twilight was just merging into night. A ray of light from the lantern at the end of the quay went trembling across the sea, and in the little harbour the dusky shapes of a few small craft lay motionless on the dark water.

The master of the schooner *Harebell* came slowly towards the harbour, accompanied by his mate. Both men had provided ashore for a voyage which included no intoxicants, and the dignity of the skipper, always a salient feature, had developed tremendously under the influence of brown stout. He stepped aboard his schooner importantly, and then, turning to the mate, who was about to follow, suddenly held up his hand for silence.

"What did I tell you?" he inquired severely as the mate got quietly aboard.

"About knocking down the two policemen?" guessed the mate, somewhat puzzled.

"No," said the other shortly. "Listen."

The mate listened. From the foc'sle came the

low gruff voices of men, broken by the silvery ripple of women's laughter.

"Well, I 'm a Dutchman," said the mate with the air of one who felt he was expected to say something.

"After all I said to 'em," said the skipper with weary dignity. "You 'eard what I said to 'em, Jack?"

"Nobody could ha' swore louder," testified the mate.

"An' here they are," said the skipper in amaze, "defying of me. After all I said to 'em. After all the threats I—I employed."

"Employed," repeated the mate with relish.

"They 've been and gone and asked them females down the foc'sle again. You know what I said I 'd do, Jack, if they did."

"Said you 'd eat 'em without salt," quoted the other helpfully.

"I 'll do worse than that, Jack," said the skipper after a moment's discomfiture. "What 's to hinder us casting off quietly and taking them along with us?"

"If you ask me," said the mate, "I should say you couldn't please the crew better."

"Well, we 'll see," said the other, nodding sagely; "don't make no noise, Jack."

He set an example of silence himself, and aided

by the mate, cast off the warps which held his unconscious visitors to their native town, and the wind being off the shore the little schooner drifted silently away from the quay.

The skipper went to the wheel, and the noise of the mate hauling on the jib brought a rough head out of the foc'sle, the owner of which, after a cry to his mates below, sprang up on deck and looked round in bewilderment.

"Stand by, there!" cried the skipper as the others came rushing on deck. "Shake 'em out."

"Beggin' your pardin', sir," said one of them with more politeness in his tones than he had ever used before, "but——"

"Stand by!" said the skipper.

"Now then!" shouted the mate sharply, "lively there! Lively with it!"

The men looked at each other helplessly and went to their posts as a scream of dismay arose from the fair beings below who, having just begun to realize their position, were coming on deck to try and improve it.

"What!" roared the skipper in pretended astonishment, "what! Gells aboard after all I said? It can't be; I must be dreaming!"

"Take us back!" wailed the damsels, ignoring the sarcasm; "take us back, captain."

"No, I can't go back," said the skipper. "You

see what comes o' disobedience, my gells. Lively there on that mains'l, d' ye hear?"

"We won't do it again," cried the girls, as the schooner came to the mouth of the harbour and they smelt the dark sea beyond. "Take us back."

"It can't be done," said the skipper cheerfully.

"It 's agin the lor, sir," said Ephraim Biddle solemnly.

"What! Taking my own ship out?" said the skipper in affected surprise. "How was I to know they were there? I 'm not going back; 'tain't likely. As they 've made their beds so they must lay on 'em."

"They ain't got no beds," said George Scott hastily. "It ain't fair to punish the gals for us, sir."

"Hold your tongue," said the skipper sharply.

"It 's agin the lor, sir," said Biddle again. "If so be they 're passengers, this ship ain't licensed to carry passengers. If so be as they 're took out agin their will, it 's abduction—I see the other day a chap had seven years for abducting one gal, three sevens—three sevens is—three sevens is—well, it 's more years than you 'd like to be in prison, sir."

"Bosh," said the skipper, "they 're stowaways,

an' I shall put 'em ashore at the first port we touch at—Plymouth."

A heartrending series of screams from the stowaways rounded his sentence, screams which gave way to sustained sobbing, as the schooner, catching the wind, began to move through the water.

"You'd better get below, my gals," said Biddle, who was the eldest member of the crew, consolingly.

"Why don't you make him take us back?" said Jenny Evans, the biggest of the three girls, indignantly.

"'Cos we can't, my dear," said Biddle reluctantly; "it's agin the lor. You don't want to see us put into prison, do you?"

"I don't mind," said Miss Evans tearfully, "so long as we get back. George, take us back."

"I can't," said Scott sullenly.

"Well, you can look for somebody else, then," said Miss Evans with temper. "You won't marry me. How much would you get if you did make the skipper put back?"

"Very likely six months," said Biddle solemnly.

"Six months would soon pass away," said Miss Evans briskly, as she wiped her eye.

"It would be a rest," said Miss Williams coaxingly.

The men not seeing things in quite the same light, they announced their intention of having nothing more to do with them, and crowding together in the bows beneath two or three blankets, condoled tearfully with each other on their misfortunes. For some time the men stood by offering clumsy consolations, but, tired at last of repeated rebuffs and insults, went below and turned in, leaving the satisfied skipper at the wheel.

The night was clear and the wind light. As the effects of his libations wore off the skipper had some misgivings as to the wisdom of his action, but it was too late to return, and he resolved to carry on.

Looking at all the circumstances of the case, he thought it best to keep the wheel in his own hands for a time, and the dawn came in the early hours and found him still at his post.

Objects began to stand out clearly in the growing light, and three dispirited girls put their heads out from their blankets and sniffed disdainfully at the sharp morning air. Then after an animated discussion they arose, and casting their blankets aside, walked up to the skipper and eyed him thoughtfully.

"As easy as easy," said Jenny Evans confidently,

as she drew herself up to her full height, and
looked down at the indignant man.

"Why, he isn't any bigger than a boy," said
Miss Williams savagely.

"Pity we didn't think of it before," said Miss
Davies. "I s'pose the crew won't help him?"

"Not they," said Miss Evans scornfully. "If
they do, we'll serve them the same."

They went off, leaving the skipper a prey to
gathering uneasiness, watching their movements
with wrinkled brow. From the forecastle and the
galley they produced two mops and a broom, and
he caught his breath sharply as Miss Evans came
on deck with a pot of white paint in one hand and
a pot of tar in the other.

"Now, girls," said Miss Evans.

"Put those things down," said the skipper in
a peremptory voice.

"Sha'n't," said Miss Evans bluntly. "You
haven't got enough on yours," she said, turning
to Miss Davies. "Don't spoil the skipper for
a ha'porth of tar."

At this new version of an old saw they laughed
joyously, and with mops dripping tar and paint on
the deck, marched in military style up to the
skipper, and halted in front of him, smiling
wickedly.

Then the heart of the skipper waxed sore faint

within him, and, with a wild yell, he summoned his trusty crew to his side.

The crew came on deck slowly, and casting furtive glances at the scene, pushed Ephraim Biddle to the front.

"Take those mops away from 'em," said the skipper haughtily.

"Don't you interfere," said Miss Evans, looking at them over her shoulder.

"Else we'll give you some," said Miss Williams bloodthirstily.

"Take those mops away from 'em!" bawled the skipper, instinctively drawing back as Miss Evans made a pass at him.

"I don't see as 'ow we can interfere, sir," said Biddle with deep respect.

"What!" said the astonished skipper.

"It would be agin the lor for us to interfere with people," said Biddle, turning to his mates, "dead agin the lor."

"Don't you talk rubbish," said the skipper anxiously. "Take 'em away from 'em. It's my tar and my paint, and——"

"You shall have it," said Miss Evans reassuringly.

"If we touched 'em," said Biddle impressively, "it'd be an assault at lor. 'Sides which, they'd probably muss us up with 'em. All we can do, sir, is to stand by and see fair play."

"Fair play!" cried the skipper dancing with rage, and turning hastily to the mate, who had just come on the scene. "Take those things away from 'em, Jack."

"Well, if it's all the same to you," said the mate, "I'd rather not be drawn into it."

"But I'd rather you were," said the skipper sharply. "Take 'em away."

"How?" inquired the mate pertinently.

"I order you to take 'em away," said the skipper. "How, is your affair."

"I'm not goin' to raise my hand against a woman for anybody," said the mate with decision. "It's no part o' my work to get messed up with tar and paint from lady passengers."

"It's part of your work to obey me, though," said the skipper, raising his voice; "all of you. There's five of you, with the mate, and only three gells. What are you afraid of?"

"Are you going to take us back?" demanded Jenny Evans.

"Run away," said the skipper with dignity. "Run away."

"I shall ask you three times," said Miss Evans sternly. "One—are you going back? Two—are you going back? Three——"

In the midst of a breathless silence she drew within striking distance, while her allies, taking up a position on either flank of the enemy, listened attentively to the instructions of their leader.

"Be careful he doesn't catch hold of the mops," said Miss Evans; "but if he does, the others are to hit him over the head with the handles. Never mind about hurting him."

"Take this wheel a minnit, Jack," said the skipper, pale but determined.

The mate came forward and took it unwillingly, and the skipper, trying hard to conceal his trepidation, walked towards Miss Evans and tried to quell her with his eye. The power of the human eye is notorious, and Miss Evans showed her sense of the danger she ran by making an energetic attempt to close the skipper's with her mop, causing him to duck with amazing nimbleness. At the same moment another mop loaded with white paint was pushed into the back of his neck. He turned with a cry of rage, and then realizing the odds against him flung his dignity to the winds and dodged with the agility of a schoolboy. Through the galley and round the masts he went with the avenging mops in mad pursuit, until breathless and exhausted he suddenly sprang on to the side and climbed frantically into the rigging.

"Coward!" said Miss Evans, shaking her weapon at him.

"Come down," cried Miss Williams. "Come down like a man."

"It's no good wasting time over *him*," said Miss Evans, after another vain appeal to the skipper's manhood. "He's escaped. Get some more stuff on your mops."

The mate, who had been laughing boisterously, checked himself suddenly, and assumed a gravity of demeanour more in accordance with his position. The mops were dipped in solemn silence, and Miss Evans approaching regarded him significantly.

"Now, my dears," said the mate, waving his hand with a deprecatory gesture, "don't be silly."

"Don't be *what?*" inquired the sensitive Miss Evans, raising her mop.

"You know what I mean," said the mate hastily. "I can't help myself."

"Well, we're going to help you," said Miss Evans. "Turn the ship round."

"You obey orders, Jack," cried the skipper from aloft.

"It's all very well for you sitting up there in peace and comfort," said the mate indignantly. "I'm not going to be tarred to please you. Come down and take charge of your ship."

"Do your duty, Jack," said the skipper, who was polishing his face with a handkerchief.

"They won't touch you. They daren't. They're afraid to."

"You're egging 'em on," cried the mate wrathfully. "I won't steer; come and take it yourself."

He darted behind the wheel as Miss Evans, who was getting impatient, made a thrust at him, and then, springing out, gained the side and rushed up the rigging after his captain. Biddle, who was standing close by, gazed earnestly at them and took the wheel.

"You won't hurt old Biddle, I know," he said, trying to speak confidently.

"Of course not," said Miss Evans emphatically.

"Tar don't hurt," explained Miss Williams.

"It's good for you," said the third lady positively. "One—two——"

"It's no good," said the mate as Ephraim came suddenly into the rigging; "you'll have to give in."

"I'm damned if I will," said the infuriated skipper. Then an idea occurred to him, and puckering his face shrewdly he began to descend.

"All right," he said shortly, as Miss Evans advanced to receive him. "I'll go back."

He took the wheel; the schooner came round before the wind, and the willing crew, letting the sheets go, hauled them in again on the port side.

"And now, my lads," said the skipper with a benevolent smile, "just clear that mess up off the decks, and you may as well pitch them mops overboard. They'll never be any good again."

He spoke carelessly, albeit his voice trembled a little, but his heart sank within him as Miss Evans, with a horrible contortion of her pretty face, intended for a wink, waved them back.

"You stay where you are," she said imperiously; "we'll throw them overboard—when we've done with them. What did you say, captain?"

The skipper was about to repeat it with great readiness when Miss Evans raised her trusty mop. The words died away on his lips, and after a hopeless glance from his mate to the crew and from the crew to the rigging, he accepted his defeat, and in grim silence took them home again.

PICKLED HERRING

THERE was a sudden uproar on deck, and angry shouts, accompanied by an incessant barking; the master of the brig *Arethusa* stopped with his knife midway to his mouth, and exchanging glances with the mate, put it down and rose to his feet.

"They're chevying that poor animal again," he said hotly. "It's scandalous."

"Rupert can take care of himself," said the mate calmly, continuing his meal. "I expect, if the truth's known, it's him's been doin' the chevying."

"You're as bad as the rest of 'em," said the skipper angrily, as a large brown retriever came bounding into the cabin. "Poor old Rupe! what have they been doin' to you?"

The dog, with a satisfied air, sat down panting by his chair, listening quietly to the subdued hubbub which sounded from the companion.

"Well, what is it?" roared the skipper, patting his favourite's head.

"It's that blasted dawg, sir," cried an angry

voice from above. "Go down and show 'im your leg, Joe."

"An' 'ave another lump took out of it, I s'pose," said another voice sourly. "Not me."

"I don't want to look at no legs while I'm at dinner," cried the skipper. "O' course the dog 'll bite you if you've been teasing him."

"There's nobody been teasing 'im," said the angry voice again. "That's the second one 'e's bit, and now Joe's goin' to have 'im killed—ain't you, Joe?"

Joe's reply was not audible, although the infuriated skipper was straining his ears to catch it.

"Who's going to have the dog killed?" he demanded, going up on deck, while Rupert, who evidently thought he had an interest in the proceedings, followed unobtrusively behind.

"I am, sir, said Joe Bates, who was sitting on the hatch while the cook bathed an ugly wound in his leg. "A dog's only allowed one bite, and he's 'ad two this week."

"He bit me on Monday," said the seaman who had spoken before. "Now he's done for hisself."

"Hold your tongue!" said the skipper angrily. "You think you know a lot about the law, Sam Clark; let me tell you a dog's entitled to have as many bites as ever he likes, so as he don't bite the same person twice."

"That ain't the way I 've 'eard it put afore," said Clark, somewhat taken back.

"He's the cutest dog breathing," said the skipper fondly, "and he knows all about it. He won't bite either of you again."

"And wot about them as 'asn't been bit yet, sir?" inquired the cook.

"Don't halloo before you 're hurt," advised the skipper. "If you don't tease him he won't bite you."

He went down to his dinner, followed by the sagacious Rupert, leaving the hands to go forward again, and to mutinously discuss a situation which was fast becoming unbearable.

"It can't go on no longer, Joe," said Clark firmly; "this settles it."

"Where is the stuff?" inquired the cook in a whisper.

"In my chest," said Clark softly. "I bought it the night he bit me."

"It's a risky thing to do," said Bates.

"'Ow risky?" asked Sam scornfully. "The dog eats the stuff and dies. Who's going to say what he died of? As for suspicions, let the old man suspect as much as he likes. It ain't proof."

The stronger mind had its way, as usual, and the next day the skipper, coming quietly on deck, was just in time to see Joe Bates throw down

a fine fat bloater in front of the now amiable
Rupert. He covered the distance between himself and the dog in three bounds, and seizing it by
the neck, tore the fish from its eager jaws and
held it aloft.

"I just caught 'im in the act!" he cried, as
the mate came on deck. "What did you give
that to my dog for?" he inquired of the con-
science-stricken Bates.

"I wanted to make friends with him," stammered the other.

"It's poisoned, you rascal, and you know it,"
said the skipper vehemently.

"Wish I may die, sir," began Joe.

"That 'll do," said the skipper harshly. "You 've
tried to poison my dog."

"I ain't," said Joe firmly.

"You ain't been trying to kill 'im with a
poisoned bloater?" demanded the skipper.

"Certainly not, sir," said Joe. "I wouldn't do
such a thing. I couldn't if I tried."

"Very good then," said the skipper; "if it's all
right you eat it, and I 'll beg your pardon."

"I ain't goin' to eat after a dog," said Joe,
shuffling.

"The dog's as clean as you are," said the
skipper. "I 'd sooner eat after him than you."

"Well, you eat it then, sir," said Bates desperately. "If it's poisoned you'll die, and I'll be 'ung for it. I can't say no fairer than that, can I?"

There was a slight murmur from the men, who stood by watching the skipper with an air of unholy expectancy.

"Well, the boy shall eat it then," said the skipper. "Eat that bloater, boy, and I'll give you sixpence."

The boy came forward slowly, and looking from the men to the skipper, and from the skipper back to the men, began to whimper.

"If you think it's poisoned," interrupted the mate, "you oughtn't to make the boy eat it. I don't like boys, but you must draw the line somewhere."

"It's poisoned," said the skipper, shaking it at Bates, "and they know it. Well, I'll keep it till we get to port, and then I'll have it analysed. And it'll be a sorry day for you, Bates, when I hear it's poisoned. A month's hard labour is what you'll get."

He turned away and went below with as much dignity as could be expected of a man carrying a mangled herring, and placing it on a clean plate, solemnly locked it up in his state-room.

For two days the crew heard no more about it, though the skipper's eyes gleamed dangerously each time that they fell upon the shrinking Bates. The weather was almost tropical, with not an air stirring, and the *Arethusa*, bearing its dread secret still locked in its state-room, rose and fell upon a sea of glassy smoothness without making any progress worth recording.

"I wish you'd keep that thing in your berth, George," said the skipper, as they sat at tea the second evening; "it puts me in a passion every time I look at it."

"I couldn't think of it, cap'n," replied the mate firmly; "it makes me angry enough as it is. Every time I think of 'em trying to poison that poor dumb creature I sort o' choke. I try to forget it."

The skipper, eyeing him furtively, helped himself to another cup of tea.

"You haven't got a tin box with a lid to it, I s'pose?" he remarked somewhat shamefacedly.

The mate shook his head. "I looked for one this morning," he said. "There ain't so much as a bottle aboard we could shove it into, and it wants shoving into something—bad, it does."

"I don't like to be beat," said the skipper, shaking his head. "All them grinning monkeys for'ard 'ud think it a rare good joke. I'd throw it overboard if it wasn't for that. We can't keep it this weather."

"Well, look 'ere; 'ere's a way out of it," said the mate. "Call Joe down, and make him keep it in the foc'sle and take care of it. That'll punish 'em all too."

"Why, you idiot, he'd lose it!" rapped out the other impatiently.

"O' course he would," said the mate; "but that's the most digernified way out of it for you. You can call 'im all sorts o' things, and abuse 'im for the rest of his life. They'll prove themselves guilty by chucking it away, won't they?"

It really seemed the only thing to be done. The skipper finished his tea in silence, and then going on deck called the crew aft and apprised them of his intentions, threatening them with all sorts of pains and penalties if the treasure about to be confided to their keeping should be lost. The cook was sent below for it, and, at the skipper's bidding, handed it to the grinning Joe.

"And mind," said the skipper as he turned away, "I leave it in your keepin', and if it's missing I shall understand that you've made away with it, and I shall take it as a sign of guilt, and act according."

The end came sooner even than he expected. They were at breakfast next morning when Joe, looking somewhat pale, came down to the cabin, followed by Clark, bearing before him an empty plate.

"Well?" said the skipper fiercely.

"It's about the 'erring, sir," said Joe, twisting his cap between his hands.

"Well?" roared the skipper again.

"It's gone, sir," said Joe, in bereaved accents.

"You mean you've thrown it away, you infernal rascal!" bellowed the skipper.

"No, sir," said Joe.

"Ah! I s'pose it walked up on deck and jumped overboard," said the mate.

"No, sir," said Joe softly. "The dog ate it, sir."

The skipper swung round in his seat and regarded him open-mouthed.

"The—dog—ate—it?" he repeated.

"Yes, sir; Clark saw 'im do it—didn't you, Clark?"

"I did," said Clark promptly. He had made his position doubly sure by throwing it overboard himself.

"It comes to the same thing, sir," said Joe sanctimoniously; "my innercence is proved just the same. You'll find the dog won't take no 'urt through it, sir. You watch 'im."

The skipper breathed hard, but made no reply.

"If you don't believe me, sir, p'raps you'd

like to see the plate where 'e licked it?" said Joe. "Give me the plate, Sam."

He turned to take it, but in place of handing it to him that useful witness dropped it and made hurriedly for the companion-ladder, and by strenuous efforts reached the deck before Joe, although that veracious gentleman, assisted from below by strong and willing arms, made a good second.

"'E 'S a nero, that's wot 'e is, sir," said the cook, as he emptied a boiler of dirty water overboard.

"A what?" said the skipper.

"A nero," said the cook, speaking very slowly and distinctly. "A nero in real life, a chap wot, speaking for all for'ard, we 're proud to have aboard along with us."

"I didn't know he was much of a swimmer," said the skipper, glancing curiously at a clumsily-built man of middle age, who sat on the hatch glancing despondently at the side.

"No more 'e ain't," said the cook, "an' that 's what makes 'im more 'eroish still in my own opinion."

"Did he take his clothes off?" inquired the mate.

"Not a bit of it," said the delighted cook; "not a pair of trowsis, nor even 'is 'at, which was sunk."

"You 're a liar, cook," said the hero, looking up for a moment.

"You didn't take your trowsis off, George?" said the cook anxiously.

"I chucked my 'at on the pavement," growled George, without looking up.

"Well, anyway, you went over the Embankment after that pore girl like a Briton, didn't you?" said the other.

There was no reply.

"Didn't you?" said the cook appealingly.

"Did you expect me to go over like a Dutchman, or wot?" demanded George fiercely.

"That's 'is modesty," said the cook, turning to the others with the air of a showman. "'E can't bear us to talk about it. Nearly drownded 'e was. All but, and a barge came along and shoved a boat-hook right through the seat of his trowsis an' saved 'im. Stand up an' show 'em your trowsis, George."

"If I do stand up," said George, in a voice broken with rage, "it 'll be a bad day for you, my lad."

"Ain't he modest?" said the cook. "Don't it do you good to 'ear 'im? He was just like that when they got him ashore and the crowd started patting him."

"Didn't like it?" queried the mate.

"Well, they overdid it a little, p'raps," admitted the cook; "one old chap wot couldn't get near patted 'is 'ead with 'is stick, but it was all meant in the way of kindness."

"I'm proud of you, George," said the skipper heartily.

"We all are," said the mate.

George grunted.

"I'll write for the medal for him," said the skipper. "Were there any witnesses, cook?"

"Heaps of 'em," said the other, "but I gave 'em 'is name and address. 'Schooner *John Henry*, of Limehouse, is 'is home,' I ses, 'and George Cooper 'is name.'"

"You talked a damned sight too much," said the hero, "you lean, lop-sided son of a tinker."

"There's 'is modesty ag'in," said the cook, with a knowing smile. "'E's busting with modesty, is George. You should ha' seen 'im when a chap took 'is fortygraph."

"Took his what?" said the skipper, becoming interested.

"His fortygraph," said the cook. "'E was a young chap what was taking views for a noose-paper. 'E took George drippin' wet just as 'e come out of the water, 'e took him arter 'e 'ad 'is face wiped, an' 'e took 'im when 'e was sitting up swearing at a man wot asked 'im whether 'e was very wet."

"An' you told 'im where I lived, and what I

was," said George, turning on him and shaking his fist. "You did."

"I did," said the cook simply. "You'll live to thank me for it, George."

The other gave a dreadful howl, and rising from the deck walked forward and went below, giving a brother seaman who patted his shoulder as he passed a blow in the ribs, which nearly broke them. Those on deck exchanged glances.

"Well, I don't know," said the mate, shrugging his shoulders; "seems to me if I'd saved a fellow-critter's life I shouldn't mind hearing about it."

"That's what you think," said the skipper, drawing himself up a little. "If ever you do do anything of the kind perhaps you'll feel different about it."

"Well, I don't see how you should know any more than me," said the other.

The skipper cleared his throat.

"There have been one or two little things in my life which I'm not exactly ashamed of," he said modestly.

"That ain't much to boast of," said the mate, wilfully misunderstanding him.

"I mean," said the skipper sharply, "one or two things which some people might have been proud of. But I'm proud to say that there isn't a living soul knows of 'em."

" I can quite believe that," assented the mate, and walked off with an irritating smile.

The skipper was about to follow him, to complain of the needless ambiguity of his remarks, when he was arrested by a disturbance from the foc'sle. In response to the cordial invitation of the cook, the mate and one of the hands from the brig *Endeavour*, moored alongside, had come aboard and gone below to look at George. The manner in which they were received was a slur upon the hospitality of the *John Henry;* and they came up hurriedly, declaring that they never wanted to see him again as long as they lived, and shouting offensive remarks behind them as they got over the side of their own vessel.

The skipper walked slowly to the foc'sle and put his head down.

" George," he shouted.

" Sir," said the hero gruffly.

" Come down into the cabin," said the other, turning away. " I want to have a little talk with you."

George rose, and, first uttering some terrible threats against the cook, who bore them with noble fortitude, went on deck and followed the skipper to the cabin.

At his superior's request he took a seat on the locker, awkwardly enough, but smiled faintly as the skipper produced a bottle and a couple of glasses.

"Your health, George," said the skipper, as he pushed a glass towards him and raised his own.

"My bes' respec's, sir," said George, allowing the liquor to roll slowly round his mouth before swallowing it. He sighed heavily, and, putting his empty glass on the table, allowed his huge head to roll on his chest.

"Saving life don't seem to agree with you, George," said the skipper. "I like modesty, but you seem to me to carry it a trifle too far."

"It ain't modesty, sir," said George; "it's that fortygraph. When I think o' that I go 'ot all over."

"I shouldn't let that worry me if I was you, George," said the. other kindly. "Looks ain't everything."

"I didn't mean it that way," said George very sourly. "My looks is good enough for me. In fact, it is partly owing to my looks, so to speak, that I'm in a mess."

"A little more rum, George?" said the skipper, whose curiosity was roused. "I don't want to know your business, far from it. But in my position as cap'n, if any of my crew gets in a mess I consider it's my duty to lend them a hand out of it, if I can."

" The world 'ud be a better place if there was more like you," said George, waxing sentimental as he sniffed delicately at the fragrant beverage. "If that noosepaper, with them pictures, gets into a certain party's 'ands, I 'm ruined."

"Not if I can help it, George," said the other with great firmness. "How do you mean ruined ?"

The seaman set his glass down on the little table, and, leaning over, formed a word with his lips, and then drew back slowly and watched the effect.

" What ? " said the skipper.

The other repeated the performance, but beyond seeing that some word of three syllables was indicated the skipper obtained no information.

" You can speak a little louder," he said somewhat crustily.

"Bigamy !" said George, breathing the word solemnly.

" You ? " said the skipper.

George nodded. "And if my first only gets hold of that paper, and sees my phiz and reads my name, I 'm done for. There's my reward for saving a fellow-critter's life. Seven years."

"I 'm surprised at you, George," said the skipper sternly. "Such a good wife as you 've got too."

"I ain't saying nothing agin number two," grumbled George. "It's number one that didn't suit. I left her eight years ago. She was a bad 'un. I took a v'y'ge to Australia furst, just to put her out o' my mind a bit, an' I never seed her since. Where am I if she sees all about me in the paper?"

"Is she what you'd call a vindictive woman?" inquired the other. "Nasty-tempered, I mean."

"Nasty-tempered," echoed the husband of two. "If that woman could only have me put in gaol she'd stand on 'er 'ead for joy."

"Well, I'll do what I can for you if the worst comes to the worst," said the skipper. "You'd better not say anything about this to anybody else."

"Not me," said George fervently, as he rose, "an' o' course you——"

"You can rely on me," said the skipper in his most stately fashion.

He thought of the seaman's confidence several times during the evening, and, being somewhat uncertain of the law as to bigamy, sought information from the master of the *Endeavour* as they sat in the latter's cabin at a quiet game of cribbage. By virtue of several appearances in the law courts with regard to collisions and spoilt cargoes this gentleman had obtained a knowledge of law which

made him a recognized authority from London
Bridge to the Nore.

It was a delicate matter for the master of the
John Henry to broach, and, with the laudable desire
of keeping the hero's secret, he approached it by a
most circuitous route.   He began with a burglary,
followed with an attempted murder, and finally
got on the subject of bigamy, *viâ* the " Deceased
Wife's Sister Bill."

" What sort o' bigamy ? " inquired the master of
the brig.   · ·

" Oh, two wives," said Captain Thomsett.

" Yes, yes," said the other, " but are there any
mitigating circumstances in the case, so that you
could throw yourself on the mercy o' the court,
I mean ? "

" *My* case ! " said Thomsett, glaring.   " It ain't
for me."

" Oh, no, o' course not," said Captain Stubbs.

" What do you mean by ' o' course not' ? "
demanded the indignant master of the *John
Henry.*

" Your deal," said Captain Stubbs, pushing the
cards over to him.

" You haven't answered my question," said
Captain Thomsett, regarding him offensively.

" There's some questions," said Stubbs slowly,
" as is best left unanswered.   When you've seen

as much law as I have, my lad, you'll know that one of the first principles of English law is, that nobody is bound to commit themselves."

"Do you mean to say you think it *is* me?" bellowed Captain Thomsett.

"I mean to say nothing," said Captain Stubbs, putting his huge hands on the table. "But when a man comes into my cabin and begins to hum an' haw an' hint at things, and then begins to ask my advice about bigamy, I can't help thinking. This is a free country, and there's no law ag'in thinking. Make a clean breast of it, cap'n, an' I'll do what I can for you."

"You're a blanked fool," said Captain Thomsett wrathfully.

Captain Stubbs shook his head gently, and smiled with infinite patience. "P'raps so," he said modestly. "P'raps so; but there's one thing I can do, and that is, I can read people."

"You can read me, I s'pose?" said Thomsett sneeringly.

"Easy, my lad," said the other, still preserving, though by an obvious effort, his appearance of judicial calm. "I've seen your sort before. One in pertikler I call to mind. He's doing fourteen years now, pore chap. But you needn't be alarmed, cap'n. Your secret is safe enough with me."

Captain Thomsett got up and pranced up and down the cabin, but Captain Stubbs remained calm. He had seen *that* sort before. It was interesting to the student of human nature, and he regarded his visitor with an air of compassionate interest. Then Captain Thomsett resumed his seat, and, to preserve his own fair fame, betrayed that of George.

"I knew it was either you or somebody your kind 'art was interested in," said the discomfited Stubbs, as they resumed the interrupted game. "You can't help your face, cap'n. When you was thinking about that pore chap's danger it was working with emotion. It misled me, I own it, but it ain't often I meet such a feeling 'art as yours."

Captain Thomsett, his eyes glowing affectionately, gripped his friend's hand, and in the course of the game listened to an exposition of the law relating to bigamy of a most masterly and complicated nature, seasoned with anecdotes calculated to make the hardiest of men pause on the brink of matrimony and think seriously of their position.

"Suppose this woman comes aboard after pore George," said Thomsett. "What's the best thing to be done?"

"The first thing," said Captain Stubbs, "is to gain time. Put her off."

"Off the ship, d' ye mean ?" inquired the other.

"No, no," said the jurist. "Pretend he's ill and can't see anybody. By gum, I 've got it."

He slapped the table with his open hand, and regarded the other triumphantly.

"Let him turn into his bunk and pretend to be dead," he continued, in a voice trembling with pride at his strategy. "It's pretty dark down your foc'sle, I know. Don't have no light down there, and tell him to keep quiet."

Captain Thomsett's eyes shone, but with a qualified admiration.

"Ain't it somewhat sudden ?" he demurred.

Captain Stubbs regarded him with a look of supreme artfulness, and slowly closed one eye.

"He got a chill going in the water," he said quietly.

"Well, you're a masterpiece," said Thomsett ungrudgingly. "I will say this of you, you're a masterpiece. Mind this is all to be kept quite secret."

"Make your mind easy," said the eminent jurist. "If I told all I know there's a good many men in this river as 'ud be doing time at the present moment."

Captain Thomsett expressed his pleasure at this information, and, having tried in vain to obtain a few of their names, even going so far as to suggest some, looked at the clock, and, shaking hands, departed to his own ship. Captain Stubbs, left to himself, finished his pipe and retired to rest; and his mate, who had been lying in the adjoining bunk during the consultation, vainly trying to get to sleep, scratched his head, and tried to think of a little strategy himself. He had glimmerings of it before he fell asleep, but when he awoke next morning it flashed before him in all the fulness of its matured beauty.

He went on deck smiling, and, leaning his arms on the side, gazed contemplatively at George, who was sitting on the deck listening darkly to the cook as that worthy read aloud from a newspaper.

"Anything interesting, cook?" demanded the mate.

"About George, sir," said the cook, stopping in his reading. "There's pictures of 'im too."

He crossed to the side, and, handing the paper to the mate, listened smilingly to the little ejaculations of surprise and delight of that deceitful man as he gazed upon the likenesses. "Wonderful," he said emphatically. "Wonderful. I never saw such a good likeness in my life, George. That'll be copied in every newspaper in London, and here's the name in full too—'George Cooper,

schooner *John Henry*, now lying off Limehouse.'"

He handed the paper back to the cook and
turned away grinning as George, unable to control
himself any longer, got up with an oath and went
below to nurse his wrath in silence. A little later
the mate of the brig, after a very confidential chat
with his own crew, lit his pipe and, with a jaunty
air, went ashore.

For the next hour or two George alternated
between the foc'sle and the deck, from whence
he cast harassed glances at the busy wharves
ashore. The skipper, giving it as his own suggestion, acquainted him with the arrangements made
in case of the worst, and George, though he seemed
somewhat dubious about them, went below and
put his bed in order.

"It's very unlikely she'll see that particular
newspaper though," said the skipper encouragingly.

"People are sure to see what you don't want
'em to," growled George. "Somebody what
knows us is sure to see it, an' show 'er."

"There's a lady stepping into a waterman's
skiff now," said the skipper, glancing at the stairs.
"That wouldn't be her, I s'pose?"

He turned to the seaman as he spoke,
but the words had hardly left his lips before

George was going below and undressing for his part.

"If anybody asks for me," he said, turning to the cook, who was regarding his feverish movements in much astonishment, "I'm dead."

"You're wot?" inquired the other.

"Dead," said George. "Dead. Died at ten o'clock this morning. D'ye understand, fat-head?"

"I can't say as 'ow I do," said the cook somewhat acrimoniously.

"Pass the word round that I'm dead," repeated George hurriedly. "Lay me out, cookie. I'll do as much for you one day."

Instead of complying the horrified cook rushed up on deck to tell the skipper that George's brain had gone; but, finding him in the midst of a hurried explanation to the men, stopped with greedy ears to listen. The skiff was making straight for the schooner, propelled by an elderly waterman in his shirt-sleeves, the sole passenger being a lady of ample proportions, who was watching the life of the river through a black veil.

In another minute the skiff bumped alongside, and the waterman standing in the boat passed the painter aboard. The skipper gazed at the fare and, shivering inwardly, hoped that George was a good actor.

"I want to see Mr. Cooper," said the lady grimly, as she clambered aboard, assisted by the waterman.

"I'm very sorry, but you can't see him, mum," said the skipper politely.

"Ho! carn't I?" said the lady, raising her voice a little. "You go an' tell him that his lawful wedded wife, what he deserted, is aboard."

"It 'ud be no good, mum," said the skipper, who felt the full dramatic force of the situation. "I'm afraid he wouldn't listen to you."

"Ho! I think I can persuade 'im a bit," said the lady, drawing in her lips. "Where is 'e?"

"Up aloft," said the skipper, removing his hat.

"Don't you give me none of your lies," said the lady, as she scanned both masts closely.

"He's dead," said the skipper solemnly.

His visitor threw up her arms and staggered back. The cook was nearest, and, throwing his arms round her waist, he caught her as she swayed. The mate, who was of a sympathetic nature, rushed below for whisky, as she sank back on the hatchway, taking the reluctant cook with her.

"Poor thing," said the skipper.

"Don't 'old 'er so tight, cook," said one of the men. "There's no necessity to squeeze 'er."

"Pat 'er 'ands," said another.

"Pat 'em yourself," said the cook brusquely, as

he looked up and saw the delight of the crew of the *Endeavour*, who were leaning over their vessel's side regarding the proceedings with much interest.

"Don't leave go of me," said the newly-made widow, as she swallowed the whisky, and rose to her feet.

"Stand by her, cook," said the skipper authoritatively.

"Ay, ay, sir," said the cook.

They formed a procession below, the skipper and mate leading; the cook with his fair burden, choking her sobs with a handkerchief, and the crew following.

"What did he die of?" she asked in a whisper broken with sobs.

"Chill from the water," whispered the skipper in response.

"I can't see 'im," she whispered. "It's so dark here. Has anybody got a match? Oh! here's some."

Before anybody could interfere she took a box from a locker, and, striking one, bent over the motionless George, and gazed at his tightly-closed eyes and open mouth in silence.

"You'll set the bed alight," said the mate in a low voice, as the end of the match dropped off.

"It won't hurt '*im*," whispered the widow tearfully.

The mate, who had distinctly seen the corpse shift a bit, thought differently.

"Nothing 'll 'urt 'im *now*," whispered the widow, sniffing as she struck another match. "Oh! if he could only sit up and speak to me."

For a moment the mate, who knew George's temper, thought it highly probable that he would, as the top of the second match fell between his shirt and his neck.

"Don't look any more," said the skipper anxiously; "you can't do him any good."

His visitor handed him the matches, and, for a short time, sobbed in silence.

"We've done all we could for him," said the skipper at length. "It 'ud be best for you to go home and lay down a bit."

"You're all very good, I'm sure," whispered the widow, turning away. "I'll send for him this evening."

They all started, especially the corpse.

"Eh?" said the skipper.

"He was a bad 'usband to me," she continued, still in the same sobbing whisper, "but I'll 'ave 'im put away decent."

"You'd better let us bury him," said the skipper. "We can do it cheaper than you can, perhaps?"

"No. I'll send for him this evening," said the lady. "Are they 'is clothes?"

"The last he ever wore," said the skipper pathetically, pointing to the heap of clothing. "There's his chest, pore chap, just as he left it."

The bereaved widow bent down, and, raising the lid, shook her head tearfully as she regarded the contents. Then she gathered up the clothes under her left arm, and, still sobbing, took his watch, his knife, and some small change from his chest, while the crew in dumb show inquired of the deceased, who was regarding her over the edge of the bunk, what was to be done.

"I suppose there was some money due to him?" she inquired, turning to the skipper.

"Matter of a few shillings," he stammered.

"I'll take them," she said, holding out her hand.

The skipper put his hand in his pocket and, in his turn, looked inquiringly at the late lamented for guidance; but George had closed his eyes again to the world, and, after a moment's hesitation, he slowly counted the money into her hand.

She dropped the coins into her pocket, and, with a parting glance at the motionless figure in the bunk, turned away. The procession made its way on deck again, but not in the same order, the cook carefully bringing up the rear.

"If there's any other little things," she said, pausing at the side to get a firmer grip of the clothes under her arm.

"You shall have them," said the skipper, who had been making mental arrangements to have George buried before her return.

Apparently much comforted by this assurance, she allowed herself to be lowered into the boat, which was waiting. The excitement of the crew of the brig, who had been watching her movements with eager interest, got beyond the bounds of all decency as they saw her being pulled ashore with the clothes in her lap.

"You can come up now," said the skipper, as he caught sight of George's face at the scuttle.

"Has she gone?" inquired the seaman anxiously.

The skipper nodded, and a wild cheer rose from the crew of the brig as George came on deck in his scanty garments, and from behind the others peered cautiously over the side.

"Where is she?" he demanded.

The skipper pointed to the boat.

"That?" said George, starting. "That? That ain't my wife."

"Not your wife?" said the skipper, staring. "Whose is she then?"

"How the devil should I know?" said George,

throwing discipline to the winds in his agitation.
"It ain't my wife."

"P'raps it's one you've forgotten," suggested
the skipper in a low voice.

George looked at him and choked. "I've
never seen her before," he replied, "s'elp me.
Call her back. Stop her."

The mate rushed aft and began to haul in the
ship's boat, but George caught him suddenly by
the arm.

"Never mind," he said bitterly; "better let her
go. She seems to know too much for me. *Somebody*'s been talking to her."

It was the same thought that was troubling
the skipper, and he looked searchingly from one
to the other for an explanation. He fancied that
he saw it when he met the eye of the mate of
the brig, and he paused irresolutely as the skiff
reached the stairs, and the woman, springing
ashore, waved the clothes triumphantly in the
direction of the schooner and disappeared.

AN INTERVENTION

THERE was bad blood between the captain and mate who comprised the officers and crew of the sailing-barge "*Swallow*"; and the outset of their voyage from London to Littleport was conducted in glum silence. As far as the Nore they had scarcely spoken, and what little did pass was mainly in the shape of threats and abuse. Evening, chill and overcast, was drawing in ; distant craft disappeared somewhere between the waste of waters and the sky, and the side-lights of neighbouring vessels were beginning to shine over the water. The wind, with a little rain in it, was unfavourable to much progress, and the trough of the sea got deeper as the waves ran higher and splashed by the barge's side.

"Get the side-lights out, and quick, you," growled the skipper, who was at the helm.

The mate, a black-haired, fierce-eyed fellow of about twenty-five, set about the task with much deliberation.

"And look lively, you lump," continued the skipper.

"I don't want none of your lip," said the mate furiously; "so don't you give me none."

The skipper yawned, and stretching his mighty frame laughed disagreeably. "You'll take what I give you, my lad," said he, "whether it's lip or fist."

"Lay a finger on me and I'll knife you," said the mate. "I ain't afraid of you, for all your size."

He put out the side-lights, casting occasional looks of violent hatred at the skipper, who, being a man of tremendous physique and rough tongue, had goaded his subordinate almost to madness.

"If you've done skulking," he cried, as he knocked the ashes out of his pipe, "come and take the helm."

The mate came aft and relieved him; and he stood for a few seconds taking a look round before going below. He dropped his pipe, and stooped to recover it; and in that moment the mate, with a sudden impulse, snatched up a hand-spike and dealt him a crashing blow on the head. Half-blinded and stunned by the blow, the man fell on his knees, and shielding his face with his hands, strove to rise. Before he could do so the mate struck wildly at him again, and with a great

cry he fell backwards and rolled heavily overboard. The mate, with a sob in his breath, gazed
wildly astern, and waited for him to rise. He
waited : minutes seemed to pass, and still the body
of the skipper did not emerge from the depths.
He reeled back in a stupor; then he gave a faint
cry as his eye fell on the boat, which was dragging
a yard or two astern, and a figure which clung
desperately to the side of it. Before he had quite
realized what had happened, he saw the skipper
haul himself on to the stern of the boat and then
roll heavily into it.

Panic-stricken at the sight, he drew his knife to
cut the boat adrift, but paused as he reflected that
she and her freight would probably be picked up
by some passing vessel. As the thought struck
him he saw the dim form of the skipper come
towards the bow of the boat and, seizing the rope,
begin to haul in towards the barge.

"Stop!" shouted the mate hoarsely; "stop! or
I'll cut you loose."

The skipper let the rope go, and the boat pulled
up with a jerk.

"I'm independent of you," the skipper shouted,
picking up one of the loose boards from the
bottom of the boat and brandishing it. "If
there's any sea on I can keep her head to it
with this. Cut away."

"If I let you come aboard," said the mate, "will you swear to let bygones be bygones?"

"No!" thundered the other. "Whether I come aboard or not don't make much difference. It'll be about twenty years for you, you murdering hound, when I get ashore."

The mate made no reply, but sat silently steering, keeping, however, a wary eye on the boat towing behind. He turned sick and faint as he thought of the consequences of his action, and vainly cast about in his mind for some means of escape.

"Are you going to let me come aboard?" presently demanded the skipper, who was shivering in his wet clothes.

"You can come aboard on my terms," repeated the mate doggedly.

"I'll make no terms with you," cried the other. "I hand you over to the police directly I get ashore, you mutinous dog. I've got a good witness in my head."

After this there was silence—silence unbroken through the long hours of the night as they slowly passed. Then the dawn came. The side-lights showed fainter and fainter in the water; the light on the mast shed no rays on the deck, but twinkled uselessly behind its glass. Then the mate turned his gaze from the wet, cheerless

deck and heaving seas to the figure in the boat
dragging behind. The skipper, who returned his
gaze with a fierce scowl, was holding his wet
handkerchief to his temple.   He removed it as
the mate looked, and showed a ghastly wound.
Still, neither of them spoke. The mate averted
his gaze, and sickened with fear as he thought
of his position; and in that instant the skipper
clutched the painter, and, with a mighty heave,
sent the boat leaping towards the stern of the
barge, and sprang on deck. The mate rose to
his feet; but the other pushed him fiercely aside,
and picking up the handspike, which lay on the
raised top of the cabin, went below. Half an
hour later he came on deck with a fresh suit of
clothes on, and his head roughly bandaged, and
standing in front of the mate, favoured him with
a baleful stare.

"Gimme that helm," he cried.

The mate relinquished it.

"You dog!" snarled the other, "to try and
kill a man when he wasn't looking, and then
keep him in his wet clothes in the boat all night.
Make the most o' your time. It 'll be many a
day before you see the sea again."

The mate groaned in spirit, but made no
reply.

"I 've wrote everything down with the time

it happened," continued the other in a voice of savage satisfaction; "an' I've locked that hand-spike up in my locker. It's got blood on it."

"That's enough about it," said the mate, turning at last and speaking thickly. "What I've done I must put up with."

He walked forward to end the discussion; but the skipper shouted out choice bits from time to time as they occurred to him, and sat steering and gibing, a gruesome picture of vengeance.

Suddenly he sprang to his feet with a sharp cry. "There's somebody in the water," he roared; "stand by to pick him up."

As he spoke he pointed with his left hand, and with his right steered for something which rose and fell lazily on the water a short distance from them.

The mate, following his outstretched arm, saw it too, and picking up a boat-hook stood ready, until they were soon close enough to distinguish the body of a man supported by a life-belt.

"Don't miss him," shouted the skipper.

The mate grasped the rigging with one hand, and leaning forward as far as possible stood with the hook poised. At first it seemed as though the object would escape them, but a touch of the helm in the nick of time just enabled the mate to reach. The hook caught in the jacket, and with great care he gradually shortened it, and drew the body close to the side.

"He's dead," said the skipper, as he fastened the helm and stood looking down into the wet face of the man. Then he stooped, and taking him by the collar of his coat dragged the streaming figure on to the deck.

"Take the helm," he said.

"Ay, ay," said the other; and the skipper disappeared below with his burden.

A moment later he came on deck again. "We'll take in sail and anchor. Sharp there!" he cried.

The mate went to his assistance. There was but little wind, and the task was soon accomplished, and both men, after a hasty glance round, ran below. The wet body of the sailor lay on a locker, and a pool of water was on the cabin floor.

The mate hastily swabbed up the water, and then lit the fire and put on the kettle; while the skipper stripped the sailor of his clothes, and flinging some blankets in front of the fire placed him upon them.

For a long time they toiled in silence, in the faint hope that life still remained in the apparently dead body.

"Poor devil!" said the skipper at length, and fell to rubbing again.

"I don't believe he's gone," said the mate, panting with his exertions. "He don't feel like a dead man."

Ten minutes later the figure stirred slightly, and the men talked in excited whispers as they worked. A faint sigh came from the lips of the sailor, and his eyes partly opened.

"It's all right, matey," said the skipper; "you lie still; we'll do the rest. Jem, get some coffee ready."

By the time it was prepared the partly drowned man was conscious that he was alive, and stared in a dazed fashion at the man who was using him so roughly. Conscious that his patient was improving rapidly, the latter lifted him in his arms and placed him in his own bunk, and proffered him some steaming hot coffee. He sipped a little, then lapsed into unconsciousness again. The two men looked at each other blankly.

"Some of 'em goes like that," said the skipper. "I've seen it afore. Just as you think they're pulling round they slip their cable."

"We must keep him warm," said the mate. "I don't see as we can do any more."

"We'll get under way again," said the other;

and pausing to heap some more clothes over the sailor he went on deck, followed by the mate; and in a short time the *Swallow* was once more moving through the water. Then the skipper, leaving the mate at the helm, went below.

Half an hour passed.

"Go and see what you can make of him," said the skipper as he re-appeared and took the helm. "He keeps coming round a bit, and then just drifts back. Seems like as if he can't hook on to life. Don't seem to take no interest in it."

The mate obeyed in silence; and for the remainder of the day the two men relieved each other at the bedside of the sailor. Towards evening, as they were entering the river which runs up to Littleport, he made decided progress under the skipper's ministrations; and the latter thrust his huge head up the hatchway and grinned in excusable triumph at the mate as he imparted the news. Then he suddenly remembered himself, and the smile faded. The light, too, faded from the mate's face.

"'Bout that mutiny and attempted murder," said the skipper, and paused as though waiting for the mate to contradict or qualify the terms; but he made no reply.

"I give you in charge as soon as we get to

port," continued the other. "Soon as the ship's berthed, you go below."

"Ay, ay," said the mate, but without looking at him.

"Nice thing it'll be for your wife," said the skipper sternly. "You'll get no mercy from me."

"I don't expect none," said the mate huskily. "What I've done I'll stand to."

The reply on the skipper's lips merged into a grunt, and he went below. The sailor was asleep, and breathing gently and regularly; and after regarding him for some time the watcher returned to the deck and busied himself with certain small duties preparatory to landing.

Slowly the light faded out of the sky, and the banks of the river grew indistinct; and one by one the lights of Littleport came into view as they rounded the last bend of the river, and saw the little town lying behind its veil of masts and rigging. The skipper came aft and took the helm from the mate, and looked at him out of the corner of his eye, as he stood silently waiting with his hands by his side.

"Take in sail," said the skipper shortly; and leaving the helm a bit, ran to assist him. Five minutes later the *Swallow* was alongside of the wharf, and then, everything made fast and snug, the two men turned and faced each other.

"Go below," said the skipper sternly. The mate walked off. "And take care of that chap. I'm going ashore. If anybody asks you about these scratches, I got 'em in a row down Wapping—D'ye hear?"

The mate heard, but there was a thickness in his throat which prevented him from replying promptly. By the time he had recovered his voice the other had disappeared over the edge of the wharf, and the sound of his retreating footsteps rang over the cobblestone quay. The mate in a bewildered fashion stood for a short time motionless; then he turned, and drawing a deep breath, went below.

THE GREY PARROT

THE Chief Engineer and the Third sat at tea on the S.S. *Curlew* in the East India Docks. The small and not over-clean steward having placed everything he could think of upon the table, and then added everything the Chief could think of, had assiduously poured out two cups of tea and withdrawn by request. The two men ate steadily, conversing between bites, and interrupted occasionally by a hoarse and sepulchral voice, the owner of which, being much exercised by the sight of the food, asked for it, prettily at first, and afterwards in a way which at least compelled attention.

"That's pretty good for a parrot," said the Third critically. "Seems to know what he's saying too. No, don't give it anything. It'll stop if you do."

"There's no pleasure to *me* in listening to coarse language," said the Chief with dignity.

He absently dipped a piece of bread and butter in the Third's tea, and losing it chased it round and round the bottom of the cup with his finger, the Third regarding the operation with an interest and emotion which he was at first unable to understand.

"You'd better pour yourself out another cup," he said thoughtfully as he caught the Third's eye.

"I'm going to," said the other dryly.

"The man I bought it of," said the Chief, giving the bird the sop, "said that it was a perfectly respectable parrot and wouldn't know a bad word if it heard it. I hardly like to give it to my wife now."

"It's no good being too particular," said the Third, regarding him with an ill-concealed grin; "that's the worst of all you young married fellows. Seem to think your wife has got to be wrapped up in brown paper. Ten chances to one she'll be amused."

The Chief shrugged his shoulders disdainfully. "I bought the bird to be company for her," he said slowly; "she'll be very lonesome without me, Rogers."

"How do you know?" inquired the other.

"She said so," was the reply.

"When you've been married as long as I have," said the Third, who having been married some fifteen years felt that their usual positions

were somewhat reversed, "you'll know that
generally speaking they're glad to get rid of
you."

"What for?" demanded the Chief in a voice
that Othello might have envied.

"Well, you get in the way a bit," said Rogers
with secret enjoyment; "you see you upset the
arrangements. House-cleaning and all that sort
of thing gets interrupted. They're glad to see
you back at first, and then glad to see the back
of you."

"There's wives and wives," said the bride-
groom tenderly.

"And mine's a good one," said the Third,
"registered A1 at Lloyd's, but she don't worry
about me going away. Your wife's thirty years
younger than you, isn't she?"

"Twenty-five," corrected the other shortly.
"You see what I'm afraid of is, that she'll get
too much attention."

"Well, women like that," remarked the Third.

"But I don't, damn it," cried the Chief hotly.
"When I think of it I get hot all over. Boiling
hot."

"That won't last," said the other reassuringly;
you won't care twopence this time next year."

"We're not all alike," growled the Chief; "some
of us have got finer feelings than others have. I

saw the chap next door looking at her as we passed him this morning.'

"Lor'," said the Third.

"I don't want any of your damned impudence," said the Chief sharply. "He put his hat on straighter when he passed us. What do you think of that?"

"Can't say," replied the other with commendable gravity; "it might mean anything."

"If he has any of his nonsense while I'm away I'll break his neck," said the Chief passionately. "I shall know of it."

The other raised his eyebrows.

"I've asked the landlady to keep her eyes open a bit," said the Chief. "My wife was brought up in the country, and she's very young and simple, so that it is quite right and proper for her to have a motherly old body to look after her."

"Told your wife?" queried Rogers.

"No," said the other. "Fact is, I've got an idea about that parrot. I'm going to tell her it's a magic bird, and will tell me everything she does while I'm away. Anything the landlady tells me I shall tell her I got from the parrot. For one thing, I don't want her to go out after seven of an evening, and she's promised me she won't. If she does I shall know, and pretend that I know through the parrot.   What do you think of it?"

"Think of it?" said the Third, staring at him. "Think of it? Fancy a man telling a grown-up woman a yarn like that!"

"She believes in warnings and death-watches, and all that sort of thing," said the Chief, "so why shouldn't she?"

"Well, you'll know whether she believes in it or not when you come back," said Rogers, "and it'll be a great pity, because it's a beautiful talker."

"What do you mean?" said the other.

"I mean it'll get its little neck wrung," said the Third.

"Well, we'll see," said Gannett.   "I shall know what to think if it does die."

"I shall never see that bird again," said Rogers, shaking his head as the Chief took up the cage and handed it to the steward, who was to accompany him home with it.

The couple left the ship and proceeded down the East India Dock Road side by side, the only incident being a hot argument between a constable and the engineer as to whether he could or could not be held responsible for the language in which the parrot saw fit to indulge when the steward happened to drop it.

The engineer took the cage at his door, and, not without some misgivings, took it upstairs into the parlour and set it on the table. Mrs. Gannett, a simple-looking woman, with sleepy brown eyes and a docile manner, clapped her hands with joy.

"Isn't it a beauty?" said Mr. Gannett, looking at it; "I bought it to be company for you while I'm away."

"You're too good to me, Jem," said his wife. She walked all round the cage admiring it, the parrot, which was of a highly suspicious and nervous disposition, having had boys at its last place, turning with her. After she had walked round him five times he got sick of it, and in a simple sailorly fashion said so.

"Oh, Jem," said his wife.

"It's a beautiful talker," said Gannett hastily, "and it's so clever that it picks up everything it hears, but it'll soon forget it."

"It looks as though it knows what you are saying," said his wife. "Just look at it, the artful thing."

The opportunity was too good to be missed, and in a few straightforward lies the engineer acquainted Mrs. Gannett of the miraculous powers with which he had chosen to endow it.

"But you don't believe it?" said his wife, staring at him open-mouthed.

"I do," said the engineer firmly.

"But how can it know what I'm doing when I'm away?" persisted Mrs. Gannett.

"Ah, that's its secret," said the engineer; "a good many people would like to know that, but nobody has found out yet. It's a magic bird, and when you've said that you've said all there is to say about it."

Mrs. Gannett, wrinkling her forehead, eyed the marvellous bird curiously.

"You'll find it's quite true," said Gannett; "when I come back that bird'll be able to tell me how you've been and all about you. Everything you've done during my absence."

"Good gracious!" said the astonished Mrs. Gannett.

"If you stay out after seven of an evening, or do anything else that I shouldn't like, that bird'll tell me," continued the engineer impressively. "It'll tell me who comes to see you, and in fact it will tell me everything you do while I'm away."

"Well, it won't have anything bad to tell of me," said Mrs. Gannett composedly, "unless it tells lies."

"It can't tell lies," said her husband confidently, "and now, if you go and put your bonnet on, we'll drop in at the theatre for half an hour."

It was a prophetic utterance, for he made such a fuss over the man next to his wife offering her his opera-glasses, that they left, at the urgent request of the management, in almost exactly that space of time.

"You'd better carry me about in a bandbox," said Mrs. Gannett wearily as the outraged engineer stalked home beside her. "What harm was the man doing?"

"You must have given him some encouragement," said Mr. Gannett fiercely—"made eyes at him or something. A man wouldn't offer to lend a lady his opera-glasses without."

Mrs. Gannett tossed her head—and that so decidedly, that a passing stranger turned his head and looked at her. Mr. Gannett accelerated his pace, and taking his wife's arm, led her swiftly home with a passion too great for words.

By the morning his anger had evaporated, but his misgivings remained. He left after breakfast for the *Curlew*, which was to sail in the afternoon, leaving behind him copious instructions, by following which his wife would be enabled to come down and see him off with the minimum exposure of her fatal charms.

Left to herself Mrs. Gannett dusted the room, until, coming to the parrot's cage, she put down the duster and eyed its eerie occupant curiously. She fancied that she saw an evil glitter in the creature's eye, and the knowing way in which it drew the film over it was as near an approach to a wink as a bird could get.

She was still looking at it when there was a knock at the door, and a bright little woman— rather smartly dressed—bustled into the room, and greeted her effusively.

"I just came to see you, my dear, because I thought a little outing would do me good," she said briskly; "and if you've no objection I'll come down to the docks with you to see the boat off."

Mrs. Gannett assented readily. It would ease the engineer's mind, she thought, if he saw her with a chaperon.

"Nice bird," said Mrs. Cluffins, mechanically bringing her parasol to the charge.

"Don't do that," said her friend hastily.

"Why not?" said the other.

"Language!" said Mrs. Gannett solemnly.

"Well, I must do something to it," said Mrs. Cluffins restlessly.

She held the parasol near the cage and suddenly opened it. It was a flaming scarlet, and for the moment the shock took the parrot's breath away.

"He don't mind that," said Mrs. Gannett

The parrot, hopping to the farthest corner of the bottom of his cage, said something feebly. Finding that nothing dreadful happened, he repeated his remark somewhat more boldly, and, being convinced after all that the apparition was quite harmless and that he had displayed his craven spirit for nothing, hopped back on his perch and raved wickedly.

"If that was my bird," said Mrs. Cluffins, almost as scarlet as her parasol, "I should wring its neck."

"No, you wouldn't," said Mrs. Gannett solemnly. And having quieted the bird by throwing a cloth over its cage, she explained its properties.

"What!" said Mrs. Cluffins, unable to sit still in her chair. "You mean to tell me your husband said that!"

Mrs. Gannett nodded.

"He's awfully jealous of me," she said with a slight simper.

"I wish he was my husband," said Mrs. Cluffins in a thin, hard voice. "I wish C. would talk to *me* like that. I wish somebody would try and persuade C. to talk to me like that."

"It shows he's fond of me," said Mrs. Gannett, looking down.

Mrs. Cluffins jumped up, and snatching the cover

off the cage, endeavoured, but in vain, to get the parasol through the bars.

' "And you believe that rubbish!" she said scathingly. "Boo, you wretch!"

"I don't believe it," said her friend, taking her gently away and covering the cage hastily just as the bird was recovering, "but I let him think do."

"I call it an outrage," said Mrs. Cluffins, waving the parasol wildly. "I never heard of such a thing; I'd like to give Mr. Gannett a piece of my mind. Just about half an hour of it. He wouldn't be the same man afterwards—I'd parrot him."

Mrs. Gannett, soothing her agitated friend as well as she was able, led her gently to a chair and removed her bonnet, and finding that complete recovery was impossible while the parrot remained in the room, took that wonder-working bird outside.

By the time they had reached the docks and boarded the *Curlew* Mrs. Cluffins had quite recovered her spirits. She roamed about the steamer asking questions, which savoured more of idle curiosity than a genuine thirst for knowledge, and was at no pains to conceal her opinion of those who were unable to furnish her with satisfactory replies.

"I shall think of you every day, Jem," said Mrs. Gannett tenderly.

"I shall think of you every minute," said the engineer reproachfully.

He sighed gently and gazed in a scandalized fashion at Mrs. Cluffins, who was carrying on a desperate flirtation with one of the apprentices.

"She's very light-hearted," said his wife, following the direction of his eyes.

"She is," said Mr. Gannett curtly, as the unconscious Mrs. Cluffins shut her parasol and rapped the apprentice playfully with the handle. "She seems to be on very good terms with Jenkins, laughing and carrying on. I don't suppose she's ever seen him before."

"Poor young things," said Mrs. Cluffins solemnly, as she came up to them. "Don't you worry, Mr. Gannett; I'll look after her and keep her from moping."

"You're very kind," said the engineer slowly.

"We'll have a jolly time," said Mrs. Cluffins. "I often wish my husband was a seafaring man. A wife does have more freedom, doesn't she?"

"More what?" inquired Mr. Gannett huskily.

"More freedom," said Mrs. Cluffins gravely. "I always envy sailors' wives. They can do as they like. No husband to look after them for nine or ten months in the year."

Before the unhappy engineer could put his indignant thoughts into words there was a warning cry from the gangway, and with a hasty farewell he hurried below. The visitors went ashore, the gangway was shipped, and in response to the clang of the telegraph the *Curlew* drifted slowly away from the quay and headed for the swing bridge slowly opening in front of her.

The two ladies hurried to the pier-head and watched the steamer down the river until a bend hid it from view. Then Mrs. Gannett, with a sensation of having lost something, due, so her friend assured her, to the want of a cup of tea, went slowly back to her lonely home.

In the period of grass widowhood which ensued, Mrs. Cluffins's visits formed almost the sole relief to the bare monotony of existence. As a companion the parrot was an utter failure, its language being so irredeemably bad that it spent most of its time in the spare room with a cloth over its cage, wondering when the days were going to lengthen a bit. Mrs. Cluffins suggested selling it, but her friend repelled the suggestion with horror, and refused to entertain it at any price, even that of the publican at the corner, who, having heard of the bird's command of language, was bent upon buying it.

"I wonder what that beauty will have to tell your husband," said Mrs. Cluffins, as they sat together one day some three months after the *Curlew's* departure.

"I should hope that he has forgotten that nonsense," said Mrs. Gannett, reddening; "he never alludes to it in his letters."

"Sell it," said Mrs. Cluffins peremptorily. "It's no good to you, and Hobson would give anything for it almost."

Mrs. Gannett shook her head. "The house wouldn't hold my husband if I did," she remarked with a shiver.

"Oh, yes, it would," said Mrs. Cluffins; "you do as I tell you, and a much smaller house than this would hold him. I told C. to tell Hobson he should have it for five pounds."

"But he mustn't," said her friend in alarm.

"Leave yourself right in my hands," said Mrs. Cluffins, spreading out two small palms and regarding them complacently. "It'll be all right, I promise you."

She put her arm round her friend's waist and led her to the window, talking earnestly. In five minutes Mrs. Gannett was wavering, in ten she had given away, and in fifteen the energetic Mrs. Cluffins was *en route* for Hobson's, swinging the cage so violently in her excitement that the parrot was reduced to holding on to its perch with claws and bill. Mrs. Gannett watched the progress from the window, and with a queer look on her face sat down to think out the points of attack and defence in the approaching fray.

A week later a four-wheeler drove up to the door, and the engineer, darting upstairs three steps at a time, dropped an armful of parcels on the floor, and caught his wife in an embrace which would have done credit to a bear. Mrs. Gannett, for reasons of which lack of muscle was only one, responded less ardently.

"Ha, it's good to be home again," said Gannett, sinking into an easy-chair and pulling his wife on his knee. "And how have you been? Lonely?"

"I got used to it," said Mrs. Gannett softly.

The engineer coughed. "You had the parrot," he remarked.

"Yes, I had the magic parrot," said Mrs. Gannett.

"How's it getting on?" said her husband, looking round. "Where is it?"

"Part of it is on the mantelpiece," said Mrs. Gannett, trying to speak calmly, "part of it is in a bonnet-box upstairs, some of it's in my pocket, and here is the remainder."

She fumbled in her pocket and placed in his hand a cheap two-bladed clasp knife.

"On the mantelpiece!" repeated the engineer staring at the knife; "in a bonnet-box!"

"Those blue vases," said his wife.

Mr. Gannett put his hand to his head. If he had heard aright one parrot had changed into a pair of vases, a bonnet, and a knife. A magic bird with a vengeance.

"I sold it," said Mrs. Gannett suddenly.

The engineer's knee stiffened inhospitably, and his arm dropped from his wife's waist. She rose quietly and took a chair opposite.

"Sold it!" said Mr. Gannett in awful tones. "Sold my parrot!"

"I didn't like it, Jem," said his wife. "I didn't want that bird watching me, and I did want the vases, and the bonnet, and the little present for you."

Mr. Gannett pitched the little present to the other end of the room.

"You see it mightn't have told the truth, Jem," continued Mrs. Gannett. "It might have told all sorts of lies about me, and made no end of mischief."

"It couldn't lie," shouted the engineer passionately, rising from his chair and pacing the room. "It's your guilty conscience that's made a coward of you. How dare you sell my parrot?"

"Because it wasn't truthful, Jem," said his wife, who was somewhat pale.

"If you were half as truthful you'd do," vociferated the engineer, standing over her. "You, you deceitful woman."

Mrs. Gannett fumbled in her pocket again, and producing a small handkerchief applied it delicately to her eyes.

I—I got rid of it for your sake," she stammered. "It used to tell such lies about you. I couldn't bear to listen to it."

"About *me!*" said Mr. Gannett, sinking into his seat and staring at his wife with very natural amazement. "Tell lies about *me!* Nonsense! How could it?"

"I suppose it could tell me about you as easily as it could tell you about me?" said Mrs. Gannett. "There was more magic in that bird than you thought, Jem. It used to say shocking things about you. I couldn't bear it."

"Do you think you're talking to a child or a fool?" demanded the engineer.

Mrs. Gannett shook her head feebly. She still kept the handkerchief to her eyes, but allowed a portion to drop over her mouth.

"I should like to hear some of the stories it told

about me—if you can remember them," said the engineer with bitter sarcasm.

"The first lie," said Mrs. Gannett in a feeble but ready voice, "was about the time you were at Genoa. The parrot said you were at some concert gardens at the upper end of the town."

One moist eye coming mildly from behind the handkerchief saw the engineer stiffen suddenly in his chair.

"I don't suppose there even is such a place," she continued.

"I—b'leve—there—is," said her husband jerkily. "I've heard—our chaps—talk of it."

"But you haven't been there?" said his wife anxiously.

"*Never!*" said the engineer with extraordinary vehemence.

"That wicked bird said that you got intoxicated there," said Mrs. Gannett in solemn accents, "that you smashed a little marble-topped table and knocked down two waiters, and that if it hadn't been for the captain of the *Pursuit*, who was in there and who got you away, you'd have been locked up. Wasn't it a wicked bird?"

"Horrible!" said the engineer huskily.

"I don't suppose there ever was a ship called the *Pursuit*," continued Mrs. Gannett.

"Doesn't sound like a ship's name," murmured Mr. Gannett.

"Well, then, a few days later it said the *Curlew* was at Naples."

"I never went ashore all the time we were at Naples," remarked the engineer casually.

"The parrot said you did," said Mrs. Gannett.

"I suppose you'll believe your own lawful husband before that damned bird?" shouted Gannett, starting up.

"Of course I didn't believe it, Jem," said his wife. "I'm trying to prove to you that the bird was not truthful, but you're so hard to persuade."

Mr. Gannett took a pipe from his pocket, and with a small knife dug with much severity and determination a hardened plug from the bowl, and blew noisily through the stem.

"There was a girl kept a fruit-stall just by the harbour," said Mrs. Gannett, "and on this evening, on the strength of having bought three-penny-worth of green figs, you put your arm round her waist and tried to kiss her, and her sweetheart, who was standing close by, tried to stab you. The parrot said that you were in such a state of terror that you jumped into the harbour and were nearly drowned."

Mr. Gannett having loaded his pipe lit it slowly

and carefully, and with tidy precision got up and deposited the match in the fireplace.

" It used to frighten me so with its stories that I hardly knew what to do with myself," continued Mrs. Gannett. " When you were at Suez——"

The engineer waved his hand imperiously.

" That's enough," he said stiffly.

" I 'm sure I don't want to have to repeat what it told me about Suez," said his wife. " I thought you 'd like to hear it, that 's all."

" Not at all," said the engineer, puffing at his pipe. " Not at all."

" But you see why I got rid of the bird, don't you ? " said Mrs. Gannett. " If it had told you untruths about me, *you* would have believed them, wouldn't you ? "

Mr. Gannett took his pipe from his mouth and took his wife in his extended arms. " No, my dear," he said brokenly, " no more than you believe all this stuff about me."

" And I did quite right to sell it, didn't I, Jem ? "

" Quite right," said Mr. Gannett with a great assumption of heartiness. " Best thing to do with it."

" You haven't heard the worst yet," said Mrs. Gannett. " When you were at Suez——"

Mr. Gannett consigned Suez to its only rival,

and thumping the table with his clenched fist, forbade his wife to mention the word again, and desired her to prepare supper.

Not until he heard his wife moving about in the kitchen below did he relax the severity of his countenance. Then his expression changed to one of extreme anxiety, and he restlessly paced the room seeking for light. It came suddenly.

"Jenkins," he gasped, "Jenkins and Mrs. Cluffins, and I was going to tell Cluffins about him writing to his wife. I expect he knows the letter by heart."

" 'TAIN'T no use waiting any longer," said Harry Pilchard, looking over the side of the brig towards the Tower stairs. " 'E's either waiting for the money or else 'e's a-spending of it. Who's coming ashore ? "

"Give 'im another five minutes, Harry," said another seaman persuasively; "it 'ud be uncommon 'ard on 'im if 'e come aboard and then 'ad to go an' get another ship's crew to 'elp 'im celebrate it."

" 'Ard on us too," said the cook honestly. "There he is ! "

The other glanced up at a figure waving to them from the stairs. " 'E wants the boat," he said, moving aft.

" No 'e don't, Steve," piped the boy. " 'E's waving you not to. He's coming in the waterman's skiff."

"Ha ! same old tale," said the seaman wisely. "Chap comes in for a bit o' money and begins to waste it directly. There's threepence gone;

clean chucked away. Look at 'im. Just look at
him!"

"'E's got the money all right," said the cook,
"there's no doubt about that. Why, 'e looks 'arf
as large again as 'e did this morning."

The crew bent over the side as the skiff approached, and the fare, who had been leaning back
in the stern with a severely important air, rose
slowly and felt in his trousers-pocket.

"There's sixpence for you, my lad," he said
pompously. "Never mind about the change."

"All right, old slack-breeches," said the waterman with effusive good-fellowship; "up you
get."

Three pairs of hands assisted the offended fare
on board, and the boy hovering round him slapped
his legs vigorously.

"Wot are you up to?" demanded Mr. Samuel
Dodds, A.B., turning on him.

"On'y dusting you down, Sam," said the boy
humbly.

"You got the money all right, I s'pose, Sammy?"
said Steve Martin.

Mr. Dodds nodded and slapped his breast-
pocket.

"Right as ninepence," he replied genially. "I've
been with my lawyer all the arternoon, pretty
near. 'E's a nice feller.

"'Ow much is it, Sam?" inquired Pilchard eagerly.

"One 'undred and seventy-three pun seventeen shillings an' ten *pence*," said the heir, noticing with much pleasure the effect of his announcement.

"Say it agin, Sam," said Pilchard in awed tones.

Mr. Dodds, with a happy laugh, obliged him. "If you'll all come down the foc'sle," he continued, "I've got a bundle o' cigars an' a drop o' something short in my pocket."

"Let's 'ave a look at the money, Sam," said Pilchard when the cigars were alight.

"Ah, let's 'ave a look at it," said Steve.

Mr. Dodds laughed again, and, producing a small canvas bag from his pocket, dusted the table with his big palm, and spread out a roll of bank-notes and a little pile of gold and silver. It was an impressive sight, and the cook breathed so hard that one note fluttered off the table. Three men dived to recover it, while Sam, alive for the first time to the responsibilities of wealth, anxiously watched the remainder of his capital.

"There's something for you to buy sweets with, my lad," he said, restored to good-humour as the note was replaced.

He passed over a small coin, and regarded with

tolerant good-humour the extravagant manifestation of joy on the part of the youth which followed. He capered joyously for a minute or two, and then taking it to the foot of the steps, where the light was better, bit it ecstatically.

"How much is it?" inquired the wondering Steve. "You do chuck your money about, Sam."

"On'y sixpence," said Sam, laughing. "I expect if it 'ad been a shillin' it 'ud ha' turned his brain."

"It ain't a sixpence," said the boy indignantly. "It's 'arf a suvrin'."

"'Arf a wot?" exclaimed Mr. Dodds with a sudden change of manner.

"'Arf a suvrin'," repeated the boy with nervous rapidity; "and thank you very much, Sam, for your generosity. If everybody was like you we should all be the better for it. The world 'ud be a different place to live in," concluded the youthful philosopher.

Mr. Dodd's face under these fulsome praises was a study in conflicting emotions. "Well, don't waste it," he said at length, and hastily gathering up the remainder stowed it in the bag.

"What are you going to do with it all, Sam?" inquired Harry.

"I ain't made up my mind yet," said Mr. Dodds deliberately. "I 'ave thought of 'ouse property."

"I don't mean that," said the other. "I mean,

wot are you going to do with it now, to take care
of it?"

"Why, keep it in my pocket," said Sam, staring.

"Well, if I was you," said Harry impressively,
"I should ask the skipper to take care of it for me.
You know wot you are when you're a bit on,
Sam."

"Wot d'yer mean?" demanded Mr. Dodds
hotly.

"I mean," said Harry hastily, "that you've got
sich a generous nature that when you've 'ad a
glass or two you're just as likely as not to give
it away to somebody."

"I know what I'm about," said Mr. Dodds with
conviction. "I'm not goin' to get on while I've
got this about me. I'm just goin' round to the
'Bull's Head,' but I shan't drink anything to
speak of myself. Anybody that likes to come
t'ave anything at my expense is welcome."

A flattering murmur, which was music to Mr.
Dodds' ear, arose from his shipmates as they went
on deck and hauled the boat alongside. The
boy was first in her, and pulling out his pocket-
handkerchief ostentatiously wiped down a seat for
Mr. Dodds.

"Understand," said that gentleman, with whom
the affair of the half-sovereign still rankled, "*your*
drink is shandygaff."

*   *   *   *   *   *

They returned to the brig at eleven o'clock, Mr. Dodds slumbering peacefully in the stern of the boat, propped up on either side by Steve and the boy.

His sleep was so profound that he declined to be aroused, and was hoisted over the side with infinite difficulty and no little risk by his shipmates.

"Look at 'im," said Harry, as they lowered him down the forecastle. "What 'ud ha' become of 'im if we hadn't been with 'im? Where would 'is money ha' been?"

"He'll lose it as sure as eggs is heggs," said Steve, regarding him intently. "Bear a hand to lift 'im in his bunk, Harry."

Harry complied, their task being rendered somewhat difficult by a slight return of consciousness in Mr. Dodds' lower limbs, which, spreading themselves out fanwise, defied all attempts to pack them in the bunk.

"Let 'em hang out then," said Harry savagely, wiping a little mud from his face. "Fancy *that* coming in for a fortin."

"'E won't 'ave it long," said the cook, shaking his head.

"Wot 'e wants is a shock," said Harry. "'Ow 'd it be when he· wakes up to tell 'im he's lost all 'is money?"

"Wot's the good o' telling 'im," demanded the cook, "when 'e's got it in his pocket?"

"Well, let's take it out," said Pilchard. "I'll hide it under my piller, and let him think he's 'ad his pocket picked."

"I won't 'ave nothing to do with it," said Steve peremptorily. "I don't believe in sich games."

"Wot do you think, cook?" inquired Harry.

"I don't see no 'arm in it," said the cook slowly; "the fright might do 'im good, p'raps."

"It might be the saving of 'im," said Harry. He leaned over the sleeping seaman, and, gently inserting his fingers in his breast-pocket, drew out the canvas bag. "There, it is, chaps," he said gaily; "an' I'll give 'im sich a fright in the morning as he won't forget in a 'urry."

He retired to his bunk, and placing the bag under his pillow, was soon fast asleep. The other men followed his example, and Steve extinguishing the lamp, the forecastle surrendered itself to sleep.

At five o'clock they were awakened by the voice of Mr. Dodds. It was a broken, disconnected sort of voice at first, like to that of a man talking in his sleep; but as Mr. Dodds' head cleared his ideas cleared with it, and in strong, forcible language straight from the heart he consigned the eyes and limbs of some person or

persons unknown to every variety of torment;
after which, in a voice broken with emotion, he
addressed himself in terms of heart-breaking
sympathy.

"Shut up, Sam," said Harry in a sleepy voice.
"Why can't you go to sleep?"

"Sleep be 'anged," said Mr. Dodds tearfully.
"I've lorst all my money."

"You're dreamin'," said Harry lightly; "pinch
yourself."

Mr. Dodds, who had a little breath left and a
few words still comparatively fresh, bestowed
them upon him.

"I tell you you haven't lorst it," said Harry.
"Don't you remember giving it to that red-'aired
woman with a baby?"

"WOT?" said the astounded Mr. Dodds.

"You give it to 'er an' told 'er to buy the baby
a bun with it," continued the veracious Mr.
Pilchard.

"Told 'er to buy the baby a bun with it?"
repeated Mr. Dodds in a dazed voice. "Told
'er to—— Wot did you let me do it for? Wot
was all you chaps standin' by an' doin' to let me
go an' do it for?"

"We did *arsk* you not to," said Steve, joining
in the conversation.

Mr. Dodds finding language utterly useless to

express his burning thoughts, sat down and madly smashed at the table with his fists.

"Wot was *you* a-doin' to let me do it?" he demanded at length of the boy. "You ungrateful little toad. You can give me that 'arf-suvrin back, d'ye hear?"

"I can't," said the boy. "I followed your example, and give it to the red-'aired woman to buy the baby another bun with."

There was a buzzing noise in Mr. Dodds' head, and the bunks and their grinning occupants went round and round.

"'Ere, 'old up, Sam," said Pilchard, shaking him in alarm. "It's all right; don't be a fool. I've got the money."

Sam stared at him blankly.

"I've got the money," repeated the seaman.

Mr. Dodds' colour came back.

"How'd you get it?" he inquired.

"I took it out of your pocket last night just to give you a lesson," said Harry severely. "Don't you never be so silly agin, Sam."

"Gimme my money," said Mr. Dodds, glaring at him.

"You might ha' lorst it, you see, Sam," continued his benefactor; "if *I* could take it, anybody else could. Let this be a lesson to you."

"If you don't gimme my money——" began Sam violently.

"It's no good trying to do 'im a kindness," said Harry to the others as he turned to his bunk. "He can go an' lose it for all I care."

He put his hand in his bunk, and then with a sudden exclamation searched somewhat hastily amongst the bedding. Mr. Dodds, watching him with a scowl, saw him take every article separately out of his bunk, and then sink down appalled on the locker.

"You 've took it, Sam — ain't — you ? " he gasped.

" Look 'ere," said Mr. Dodds, with ominous quietness, " when you 've done your little game."

"It's gone," said Harry in a scared voice; "somebody's taken it."

"Look 'ere, 'Arry, give 'im his money," said Steve impatiently ; "a joke's a joke, but we don't want too much of it."

"I ain't got it," said Harry, trembling. "Sure as I stand 'ere it's gone. I took it out of your pocket, and put it under my piller. You saw me, didn't you, Steve? "

"Yes, and I told you not to," said Steve. "Let this be a warning to you not to try and teach lessons to people wot don't want 'em."

"I'm going to the police-station to give 'im in charge," said Mr. Dodds fiercely; "that's wot I'm goin' to do."

"For the Lord's sake don't do that, Sam," said Pilchard, clutching him by the coat.

"'Arry ain't made away with it, Sam," said Steve. "I saw somebody take it out of his bunk while he was asleep."

"Why didn't you stop him?" cried Harry, starting up.

"I didn't like to interfere," said Steve simply; "but I saw where he went to."

"Where?" demanded Mr. Dodds wildly. "Where?"

"He went straight up on deck," said Steve slowly, "walked aft, and then down into the cabin. The skipper woke up, and I heard 'im say something to him."

"Say something to 'im?" repeated the bewildered Dodds. "Wot was it?"

"Well, I 'ardly like to repeat it," said Steve, hesitating.

"Wot was it?" roared the overwrought Mr. Dodds.

"Well, I 'eard this chap say something," said Steve slowly, "and then I heard the skipper's voice. But I don't like to repeat wot 'e said, I reely don't."

"Wot was it?" roared Mr. Dodds, approaching him with clenched fist.

"Well, if you will have it," said Steve, with a little cough, "the old man said to me, 'Well done, Steve,' he ses, 'you're the only sensible man of the whole bilin' lot. Sam's a fool,' 'e ses, 'and 'Arry's worse, an' if it wasn't for men like you, Steve, life wouldn't be worth living.' The skipper's got it now, Sam, and 'e's goin' to give it to your wife to take care of as soon as we get home."

THE LOST SHIP

O N a fine spring morning in the early part of the present century, Tetby, a small port on the east coast, was keeping high holiday. Tradesmen left their shops, and labourers their work, and flocked down to join the maritime element collected on the quay.

In the usual way Tetby was a quiet, dull little place, clustering in a tiny heap of town on one side of the river, and perching in scattered red-tiled cottages on the cliffs of the other.

Now, however, people were grouped upon the stone quay, with its litter of fish-baskets and coils of rope, waiting expectantly, for to-day the largest ship ever built in Tetby, by Tetby hands, was to start upon her first voyage.

As they waited, discussing past Tetby ships, their builders, their voyages, and their fate, a small piece of white sail showed on the noble barque from her moorings up the river. The groups on the quay grew animated as more sail was set, and in a slow and stately fashion the new ship drew near. As the light breeze took her sails she came faster, sitting the water like a duck, her lofty masts tapering away to the sky as they broke through the white clouds of canvas. She passed within ten fathoms of the quay, and the men cheered and the women held their children up to wave farewell, for she was manned from captain to cabin boy by Tetby men, and bound for the distant southern seas.

Outside the harbour she altered her course somewhat and bent, like a thing of life, to the wind blowing outside. The crew sprang into the rigging and waved their caps, and kissed their grimy hands to receding Tetby. They were answered by rousing cheers from the shore, hoarse and masculine, to drown the lachrymose attempts of the women.

They watched her until their eyes were dim, and she was a mere white triangular speck on the horizon. Then, like a melting snowflake, she vanished into air, and the Tetby folk, some envying the bold mariners, and others thankful that their lives were cast upon the safe and pleasant shore, slowly dispersed to their homes.

Months passed, and the quiet routine of Tetby went on undisturbed. Other craft came into port and, discharging and loading in an easy,

comfortable fashion, sailed again. The keel of
another ship was being laid in the shipyard, and
slowly the time came round when the return of
Tetby's Pride, for so she was named, might be
reasonably looked for.

It was feared that she might arrive in the night—
the cold and cheerless night, when wife and child
were abed, and even if roused to go down on to the
quay would see no more of her than her sidelights
staining the water, and her dark form stealing
cautiously up the river. They would have her
come by day. To see her first on that horizon,
into which she had dipped and vanished. To see
her come closer and closer, the good stout ship
seasoned by southern seas and southern suns, with
the crew crowding the sides to gaze at Tetby, and
see how the children had grown.

But she came not. Day after day the watchers
waited for her in vain. It was whispered at length
that she was overdue, and later on, but only by
those who had neither kith nor kin aboard of her,
that she was missing.

Long after all hope had gone wives and mothers,
after the manner of their kind, watched and waited
on the cheerless quay. One by one they stayed
away, and forgot the dead to attend to the living.
Babes grew into sturdy, ruddy-faced boys and
girls, boys and girls into young men and women,

but no news of the missing ship, no word from the missing men. Slowly year succeeded year, and the lost ship became a legend. The man who had built her was old and grey, and time had smoothed away the sorrows of the bereaved.

It was on a dark, blustering September night that an old woman sat by her fire knitting. The fire was low, for it was more for the sake of company than warmth, and it formed an agreeable contrast to the wind which whistled round the house, bearing on its wings the sound of the waves as they came crashing ashore.

"God help those at sea to-night," said the old woman devoutly, as a stronger gust than usual shook the house.

She put her knitting in her lap and clasped her hands, and at that moment the cottage door opened. The lamp flared and smoked up the chimney with the draught, and then went out. As the old woman rose from her seat the door closed.

"Who's there?" she cried nervously.

Her eyes were dim and the darkness sudden, but she fancied she saw something standing by the door, and snatching a spill from the mantelpiece she thrust it into the fire, and relit the lamp.

A man stood on the threshold, a man of middle age, with white drawn face and scrubby beard. His clothes were in rags, his hair unkempt, and his light grey eyes sunken and tired.

The old woman looked at him, and waited for him to speak. When he did so he took a step towards her, and said—

" Mother ! "

With a great cry she threw herself upon his neck and strained him to her withered bosom, and kissed him. She could not believe her eyes, her senses, but clasped him convulsively, and bade him speak again, and wept, and thanked God, and laughed all in a breath.

Then she remembered herself, and led him tottering to the old Windsor chair, thrust him in it, and quivering with excitement took food and drink from the cupboard and placed before him. He ate hungrily, the old woman watching him, and standing by his side to keep his glass filled with the home-brewed beer. At times he would have spoken, but she motioned him to silence and bade him eat, the tears coursing down her aged cheeks as she looked at his white famished face.

At length he laid down his knife and fork, and drinking off the ale, intimated that he had finished.

" My boy, my boy," said the old woman in

a broken voice, " I thought you had gone down with *Tetby's Pride* long years ago."

He shook his head heavily.

"The captain and crew, and the good ship," asked his mother. "Where are they?"

"Captain — and — crew," said the son, in a strange hesitating fashion; "it is a long story —the ale has made me heavy. They are——"

He left off abruptly and closed his eyes.

"Where are they?" asked his mother. "What happened?"

He opened his eyes slowly.

"I—am—tired—dead tired. I have not— slept. I 'll tell—you—morning."

He nodded again, and the old woman shook him gently.

"Go to bed then. Your old bed, Jem. It's as you left it, and it's made and the sheets aired. It's been ready for you ever since."

He rose to his feet, and stood swaying to and fro. His mother opened a door in the wall, and taking the lamp lighted him up the steep wooden staircase to the room he knew so well. Then he took her in his arms in a feeble hug, and kissing her on the forehead sat down wearily on the bed.

The old woman returned to her kitchen, and falling upon her knees remained for some time in a state of grateful, pious ecstasy. When she arose she thought of those other women, and, snatching a shawl from its peg behind the door, ran up the deserted street with her tidings.

In a very short time the town was astir. Like a breath of hope the whisper flew from house to house. Doors closed for the night were thrown open, and wondering children questioned their weeping mothers. Blurred images of husbands and fathers long since given over for dead stood out clear and distinct, smiling with bright faces upon their dear ones.

At the cottage door two or three people had already collected, and others were coming up the street in an unwonted bustle.

They found their way barred by an old woman.—a resolute old woman, her face still working with the great joy which had come into her old life, but who refused them admittance until her son had slept. Their thirst for news was uncontrollable, but with a swelling in her throat she realized that her share in *Tetby's Pride* was safe.

Women who had waited, and got patient at last after years of waiting, could not endure these additional few hours. Despair was endurable, but suspense! "Ah, God! Was their man alive? What did he look like? Had he aged much?"

"He was so fatigued he could scarce speak," said she. She had questioned him, but he was unable to reply. Give him but till the dawn, and they should know all.

So they waited, for to go home and sleep was impossible. Occasionally they moved a little way up the street, but never very far, and gathering in small knots excitedly discussed the great event. It came to be understood that the rest of the crew had been cast away on an uninhabited island, it could be nothing else, and would doubtlessly soon be with them; all except one or two perhaps, who were old men when the ship sailed, and had probably died in the meantime. One said this in the hearing of an old woman whose husband, if alive, would be in extreme old age, but she smiled peacefully, albeit her lip trembled, and said she only expected to hear of him, that was all.

The suspense became almost unendurable. "Would this man never awake? Would it never be dawn?" The children were chilled with the wind, but their elders would scarcely have felt an Arctic frost. With growing impatience they waited, glancing at times at two women who held themselves somewhat aloof from the others;

two women who had married again, and whose second husbands waited, awkwardly enough, with them.

Slowly the weary windy night wore away, the old woman, deaf to their appeals, still keeping her door fast. The dawn was not yet, though the oft-consulted watches announced it near at hand. It was very close now, and the watchers collected by the door. It was undeniable that things were seen a little more distinctly. One could see better the grey, eager faces of his neighbours.

They knocked upon the door, and the old woman's eyes filled as she opened it and saw those faces. Unasked and unchid they invaded the cottage and crowded round the door.

"I will go up and fetch him," said the old woman.

If each could have heard the beating of the others' hearts, the noise would have been deafening, but as it was there was complete silence, except for some overwrought woman's sob.

The old woman opened the door leading to the room above, and with the slow, deliberate steps of age ascended the stairs, and those below heard her calling softly to her son.

Two or three minutes passed and she was heard descending the stairs again—alone. The smile, the pity, had left her face, and she seemed dazed and strange.

"I cannot wake him," she said piteously. "He sleeps so sound. He is fatigued. I have shaken him, but he still sleeps."

As she stopped, and looked appealingly round, the other old woman took her hand, and pressing it led her to a chair. Two of the men sprang quickly up the stairs. They were absent but a short while, and then they came down like men bewildered and distraught. No need to speak. A low wail of utter misery rose from the women, and was caught up and repeated by the crowd outside, for the only man who could have set their hearts at rest had escaped the perils of the deep, and died quietly in his bed.

THE END.

PLYMOUTH
WILLIAM BRENDON AND SON
PRINTERS